# THE DUKE'S WARD

Major Richard Sinclair unexpectedly finds himself the heir to a dukedom, and therefore responsible for a widowed duchess and her three daughters. With no intention of permanently burdening himself with this new inheritance, he will visit, set things in order, and then return to his military duties. Or so he thinks . . . Lady Amanda Sinclair has been managing the household since her father's demise. Can a true aristocrat like her ever teach a rough soldier how to be a successful duke?

# THE DUKE'S WARD

Major Richard Sinclair unexpectedly finds himself the heir to a dukedom, and therefore responsible for a widowed duchess and her three daughters. With no intention of permanently burdening himself with this new inheritance, he will visit, set things in order, and then return to his military duties. Or so he thinks ... Lady Amanda Sinclair has been managing the household since her father's demise. Can a true aristocrat like her ever teach a rough soldier how to be a successful duke?

# FENELLA J. MILLER

# THE DUKE'S WARD

*Complete and Unabridged*

# LINFORD
*Leicester*

First published in Great Britain in 2019

First Linford Edition
published 2020

A catalogue record for this book is available
from the British Library.

ISBN 978–1–4448–4524–2

Published by
Ulverscroft Limited
Anstey, Leicestershire

Set by Words & Graphics Ltd.
Anstey, Leicestershire
Printed and bound in Great Britain by
T. J. International Ltd., Padstow, Cornwall

This book is printed on acid-free paper

# 1

*December 1808, Spain*

A musket ball ricocheted against the wall and Major Richard Sinclair flinched. He was pressed hard against the side of an abandoned cottage. He coughed and wiped his mouth. The enemy skirmishers had pinned him and his sergeant into a corner. If his battalion didn't arrive in the next few minutes, they were done for.

He wasn't used to retreating, not in battle or in life. This forced march through Spain was a desperate attempt to reach Corunna where the ships were waiting to evacuate the troops back to England. It was the very devil. More men had been lost to the weather than to any French soldier.

Lieutenant-General Sir John Moore had marshalled his men, and if it hadn't

1

been for his bravery, more would have perished. Despite the atrocious conditions, so far Richard had lost none of his battalion to the elements.

'Major, sir, we ain't going to get out of here easy like. No sign of assistance, neither. I reckon the men have marched on and ain't noticed we're missing.'

Sergeant-Major Riley had been obliged to put his mouth adjacent to Richard's ear in order to make himself heard. 'We'll have to make a run for it. If we can climb over the wall without being hit, I think we've got a chance. Are you ready?'

'Yes, sir. I think the buggers will rush us any minute.'

The wall to which he'd referred was more than six feet in height, a few inches shorter than his sergeant and himself, so he could see that on the other side was a steep slope covered in thickets and scrub. There were trees at the bottom which would provide the necessary cover to enable them to make good their escape.

Richard steadied his breathing, reached out with one hand and gripped the top of the stonework. Then, in one fluid movement, he hauled himself up and rolled to the other side. His sergeant landed beside him. His breath hissed through his teeth. They were unscathed — nothing short of a damned miracle.

He pounded down the hill but, as he gathered speed, he lost control of his feet. His boot snagged in a bush. He completed the remainder of the journey somersaulting painfully, then staggered to his feet, bruised and bleeding, but relatively unharmed.

Riley had managed to remain upright and was having difficulty keeping his amusement hidden. 'You all right, Major? Took a nasty tumble there, you did.'

'Less talking, more running. We're sitting ducks if we remain where we are.'

They were in the safety of the woods when the musket fire resumed, and he prayed the pursuing Frenchmen would abandon their chase. Those soldiers were not as disciplined as the English, and would take the easiest way forward when they could.

They jogged in single file and silence through the trees. It was marginally warmer beneath the naked branches, but if they didn't rejoin the column before dark, they would be in trouble. Being out here without heat and food overnight might well prove fatal.

'I reckon I can hear the column, Major; it ain't no more than a mile or two ahead.'

Richard stopped and listened. Yes — his sergeant was correct. 'If we take it at the double, Riley, we'll arrive long before dark.'

They were both tired, but the exertion had at least kept them warm. He was fortunate that he had a thick greatcoat on over his uniform; his sergeant wasn't so lucky. However, he'd found a thick horse blanket, cut a slit in

4

the top, and then dropped it over his head.

They were greeted with cheers and shouts of recognition when they caught up with the battalion. Lieutenant Howard raced to his side. 'Thank God you're here, sir, I was in two minds over whether we should turn back for you, but decided against it. I hope I made the right decision.'

He clapped the young man on the shoulder. 'You did indeed. The men are fatigued; better they kept going.' He pointed to a rocky outcrop a mile ahead. 'We'll make camp there. The men will have shelter from the biting wind, and there's a stand of trees where they can find firewood.'

There would only be water and hard biscuit, but at least they could get warm. His sergeant usually managed to find him something more palatable, but he was content to eat whatever his men had. A few flakes of snow began to fall as he sat leaning against the rock face, cradling a tin mug of weak tea in his hands. God knew where Riley had found that, but it was much appreciated.

In the darkness he could see the glow of dozens of campfires. No doubt any Frenchies following would also see them. 'Riley, is there still a pursuit, do you think?'

'I sent a couple of skirmishers to investigate, sir, and they reported that they saw no sign of an encampment. I reckon they've given up and are content to leave us to battle with the weather.'

'I pray to God that you don't find any of my men frozen stiff in the morning.'

Two of his young lieutenants approached and saluted — hardly necessary in the circumstances. 'Major Sinclair, sir, sentries are in position and will be changed every four hours as instructed.'

'Excellent. Try and get some sleep between shifts, gentlemen. We have a long and difficult few days ahead of us, and I've no intention of losing any of you.'

They vanished into the darkness, leaving him alone with his sergeant. 'My main concern, Riley, is that the ships will leave without us and we'll be marooned in Corunna for the winter.'

'The young gentleman what went ahead on your horse should be back in the morning with news. An officer shouldn't be walking, you should be riding like a proper gentleman.'

'Get some sleep, Sergeant, but for God's sake keep the fire going.' Richard rolled himself up in his greatcoat and used his haversack for a pillow.

The next morning, he got up stiff and cold, and was delighted to see there'd been no further snow. The sky was clear and blue, the wind had dropped, and it was perfect marching weather. Well — as perfect as the elements could be at the beginning of December.

★ ★ ★

7

Three days later they caught up with the tail-end of the army. They were greeted with raucous shouts from those who saw them. Richard had now regained the use of his mount and rode ahead to find his commanding officer.

'Well done, Sinclair, well done indeed. How many men did you lose to the cold?'

'Three, and they were already sickening for something. We buried them. And you, sir?'

'Too damn many. Lost more to the weather than I did to the Frenchies. I'm riding ahead to the port to ensure there's sufficient room in the ships to take everyone. It's a damned horrible sea crossing, but at least we should be home for the festive season.'

Richard rode on, satisfied he'd completed his task with honour. It would be good to be back in England, although he had no family, no home of his own, to return to. He was an only child and his mother had died at his birth. His father had never forgiven him for the loss of his beloved wife, and Richard had been left to the care of servants until he was old enough to be packed off to school.

He'd shed no tears when he'd received the letter telling him of the demise of his remaining parent. To his surprise, there'd been a sizeable inheritance, which he had yet to claim. He couldn't resign his commission in the middle of a war, but when Boney was defeated he would return to civilian life and buy himself a tidy estate, find himself a pretty bride, and live the life of a country gentleman.

He would leave his three lieutenants and Sergeant-Major Riley to take care of the brigade. He would find himself a billet for the next few nights: it appeared they would not be embarking immediately as the weather had worsened. There was a fierce storm battering the harbour, making it impossible for any vessel to leave safely.

★ ★ ★

That night he sat with the other officers, drinking a decent claret in the modest sitting room of the house that had been reserved for them, content with his lot.

'I say, Sinclair, there was a scholarly gentleman enquiring after you. Did he find you?' Lord Christopher Rowley, better known to his friends as Kit, asked as he drained his fourth glass.

'Did he say why he wanted to find me?'

One of the other officers waved his glass in the air. 'Come to dun you for your debts, has he?'

Richard pushed himself to his feet. 'Unlike you, you buffoon, I have none. I pay my way.' He nodded around the circle of semi-inebriated gentlemen. 'Excuse me, I'd better go in search of this person, for I'll not sleep soundly until I discover why he's searching for me.'

He could think of only one possible reason, and that was that the lawyers who'd informed him of his inheritance had become impatient with getting no response. This seemed unlikely as, even if he had kicked the bucket, he had no heirs who would be clamouring to inherit.

He pulled his shako down over his ears and turned his collar up. His muffler covered his nose and mouth, and kept the worst of the biting wind at bay. This Spanish port was overrun with military. He sincerely hoped none of his men ended up on a charge for being drunk and disorderly. He'd heard tell of the most appalling behaviour after they'd driven the Spanish from Portugal — to think that English soldiers had looted, raped and murdered innocent civilians made his blood boil. Many of those concerned had been apprehended and hanged. Hopefully, that would be warning enough to keep his men from behaving like savages.

The last time this mystery gentleman had been seen making enquiries was at the disembarkation point. He would start there, and was determined not to retire until he'd discovered why a stranger was seeking him so urgently.

# 2

*December 1808, Suffolk, England*

'Amanda, I am in despair. We cannot possibly pay these demands this quarter. I cannot for the life of me imagine where the money has gone, or how it has gone so quickly.'

'Mama, you know very well that spending so much on frills and furbelows was an unwise decision. I warned you that this year would end in disaster for us if we did not retrench. You have chosen to ignore my advice.'

Amanda was well aware that anything she said to her mother on the subject of finance would be ignored. Since Papa had died from an apoplexy two years ago, they had been living in straitened circumstances. Until the new Duke of Denchester could be found to take up the reins of the estate, they were obliged to live from hand to mouth. The wretched lawyers wouldn't release any funds, apart from the quarterly rents from the estate. They had no access to the vast amount that was now languishing in the hands of the banks with which her father had dealt.

Her mother waved her hands as if dismissing her daughter. 'Anyway, my love, no one is going to press us to pay — they are well aware that, once the duke is here, everything will be paid. Denchester Hall has been home to the Sinclair family for hundreds of years . . .'

'That's all very well, but tradespeople have to feed their families, and I'm not prepared to keep living on their charity. We have the quarterly rents, and that would be more than sufficient to keep us fed and clothed, to pay the wages of our staff, if you had behaved as you should.'

'I cannot allow my daughters or myself to promenade in public wearing last year's fashions. We are the most important family in the neighbourhood — indeed, I believe I am the only duchess in Suffolk. It behoves us to keep up appearances, whatever you might think to the contrary.'

'That is not why I came to see you, Mama. I told you weeks ago that we cannot afford to live in this vast place any longer.'

'I misremember hearing such a thing. Where are your sisters? I have not set eyes on them this age.'

'As you very well know, today is the day that we all transfer to the Dower House. If you took the slightest interest in what was going on around you, you would have noticed that holland covers have been placed on the furniture in all the reception rooms apart from this one.'

Her mother's eyes rounded. 'I am not going to leave my home on your say-so. I am a duchess, and intend to remain here as my position demands.'

Amanda stood up. 'My sisters have already departed. Their belongings were transferred yesterday, as were mine. Your abigail will have completed your packing, and your trunks are going to be removed forthwith.' She hated to speak so firmly to her parent but, with no head of the household to take over such decisions, it was left to her to keep the family from ruin.

She scooped up the latest pile of bills from the side table upon which Mama had strewn them. 'This place is too big, too cold, and too expensive to run. I promise you we'll be more comfortable in the Dower House.'

Her mother sniffed loudly and dabbed at her eyes with a dainty lace handkerchief. 'You are a bully, Amanda. Like your father, you have no regard for a person's sensibilities. I shall come with you because I have no option but to do so.' She pushed herself upright. 'However, I do assure you that I shall not enjoy my new home one jot.'

★ ★ ★

16

The Dower House was situated a few hundred yards from the main edifice. It had been thoroughly cleaned and aired, and would be ideal for the four of them. What her mother didn't understand was that, as the Dowager Duchess of Denchester, she no longer had the right to occupy the Hall. Whoever the duke might be, he could very well be married and have a family of his own and not wish to share his home with them.

It was a mystery and concern to her that, two years since the demise of her father, the lawyers had yet to find the man who had inherited the title and the vast fortune that went with it. She had been assured there was a direct line of descent from her great-grandfather to one Richard Sinclair. This gentleman's connection to the family was via a younger brother.

Her sister Sarah was waiting eagerly to greet them in the modest entrance hall. 'Amanda, I cannot tell you how much I like this place despite my reservations,' she said. 'It is warmer, and more than adequate for our needs. We should have moved here months ago.'

'Indeed, we should. I'm counting on you, sister, to convince our mother I have made the right decision for us all. Where is Beth? Is she very disturbed by the change of circumstances?'

'Nanny has taken her to the nursery floor, and she's happily arranging her dolls.'

Amanda's sister Beth, who was seventeen years of age, was the image of their mother and had her golden curls and bright blue eyes. She was sweet-natured but, sadly, lacked intelligence. Sarah, at eighteen, was equally beautiful, and her dearest friend. Unfortunately, the fair curls and periwinkle eyes of her sisters had not been passed on to Amanda. She was, so she had been told on many occasions, the image of her father. He had been tall and broad-shouldered, but could not have been called handsome by any stretch of the imagination. His saving grace had been his nut-brown hair and pale green eyes.

The garrulous voice of their mother interrupted the conversation. 'Am I to be ignored in this way? Where is Foster? Where is Jennings? Are we not to have a butler or housekeeper at this inferior establishment?'

'They have remained at the Hall in order to organise a thorough clean of the place, so that it's in order when its new occupant eventually arrives. The senior footman, Smith, will act as butler here; and the under-housekeeper, Bentley, will assume the duties of housekeeper. I'm sure you'll not find them wanting in their duties.'

'I cannot remember ever having set foot in this house before. Direct me to the drawing room, Amanda.'

'You'll find it through those double doors to the right of you. Refreshments will be brought directly. Are you not to go upstairs and remove your outer garments first?'

'Reynolds can tend to that when she arrives. No doubt it will be unpleasantly chill in the drawing room, so keeping on my hat and pelisse is of no consequence.'

Mama had not taken this change of circumstances well, but at least she was now *in situ*. Amanda had half-a-dozen letters to peruse, and intended to take care of business before she joined her parent in the perfectly warm and pleasant drawing room.

★ ★ ★

The family did not regroup until dinner which was served at five o'clock. Amanda had ordered a simple repast, no removes and only three courses. No doubt mama would complain about this too. At least she had good news to share with them and there had been very little of that these past two years.

When they were settled and drinking their soup, she thought she would make her announcement. 'I heard from

20

London today. The head of the family, one Major Richard Sinclair, now his grace the Duke of Denchester, has finally been located.'

'At last! Where has he been for so long? Why has he ignored his responsibilities? Your departed father must be turning in his grave at such dereliction of duty.'

'Is he to arrive before Christmas, Amanda? That's only just over three weeks away,' Sarah said. Beth continued to drink her soup.

'That I do not know for sure, but I think it fairly certain we'll not see him until the new year at the earliest. He's with the army in Spain, awaiting a ship to bring him back to England.'

This was not a complete fabrication, but neither was it the absolute truth. It was better that they didn't know the full story. His grace had not in fact been told directly of his elevation — the lawyers had merely said they now knew where he was, and were sending a clerk with a letter to

Corunna in the hope of locating him.

From what she had read in *The Times*, the retreat from Napoleon's army in the most appalling weather conditions had proved disastrous for the English troops. Hundreds had succumbed to the cold, and the French were still harrying the soldiers. She prayed fervently that her very distant cousin Richard would make it safely to the port.

*December 1808, Corunna, Spain*

Richard had had a wasted journey to the port, and got wet and frozen, which did nothing for his temper. He was striding back to his billet when he heard someone hurrying along behind him. Instinctively he drew his sword and held it by his side, concealed under his coat.

'Major Sinclair, I beg you, slow your pace for I cannot walk as fast as you.'

He rammed his sword back into the

scabbard and turned to meet the clerical gentleman who had been searching for him these past few days.

'I am Sinclair. To whom am I speaking?'

A sudden gust of wind blew the man's hat from his head. Richard caught it as it flew past and handed it back with a smile.

'Thank you. Is there somewhere more convivial we can retire to? I have the most urgent business with you.'

'The house that we've requisitioned for the week is just ahead. Accompany me there: I have a chamber to myself where we can converse without interruption.'

He didn't bother to remove his outer garments, but escorted his companion up the stairs to his room before they could be waylaid by the drunken rabble in the drawing room.

'Here, sir, allow me to take your cloak. If I hang it by the fire, it will dry before you leave.'

The gentleman, about his own age

but a head shorter and half his weight, handed him the sodden garment with relief.

'I am chilled to the marrow, Major, and was beginning to despair of ever finding you.'

'Take that chair, I'll sit on this stool . . . '

'No, that will not do.'

Before he could argue the point, the man took the stool, leaving him the only chair.

'I am agog with curiosity, sir,' Richard began, 'to know why you wish to speak to me. However, before you reveal your purpose you have yet to tell me your name.'

'I am Caleb Adkin . . . ' The man hesitated, and then blurted out the most extraordinary thing. 'You have inherited the dukedom of Denchester, in Suffolk. You are in direct line of descent from your greatgrandfather, Lord Richard Sinclair, who was the youngest son.'

'God's teeth! What do I want with

such nonsense? I'm a soldier, I have no wish to become an aristocrat, and certainly not a duke. You must find someone else — I'm sure there are others with a better claim.'

'Indeed, there are not, your grace. The previous Duke of Denchester died two years ago, and the Dowager Duchess and her daughters have been obliged to move into the Dower House as they do not have access to more than the quarterly rents. They have suffered grievously with the deprivation of their usual standard of living.'

'Good God, man, that's hardly a deprivation. They should try living as my soldiers do to understand the meaning of the word. I have no time for aristocrats. Find someone else — I shall speak to the lawyers on my return and renounce the title.'

'That is your prerogative, your grace — but could I prevail upon you to act as head of the family, at least until this can be arranged? The Dowager Duchess of Denchester and her three daughters have been rudderless for two years. If you visited, you could make the arrangements for them to have access to the vast fortune that has been held back.'

'I might not be in England for weeks — but then, neither will you. Very well, if I can get leave to do so from Horse Guards, I will make a short stay at this place and ensure the ladies are taken care of.'

'Thank you, your grace. I shall send a letter to that effect immediately.' The man scrambled to his feet and bowed almost in half. 'Excuse me, I must set things in motion immediately. The storm could abate at any moment, and I wish to get this missive taken on the next ship that leaves port.'

'Before you go, tell me — what age are these daughters?'

'None have reached their majority, your grace, and all need to be presented at court in order to find a suitable husband.'

'I'm sure they can organise that for

themselves. I've no experience of the *ton*, and would rather have my teeth pulled than prance about in a hot, malodorous ballroom doing the pretty to aristos and simpering debutantes.'

'I shall bid you good night, your grace. I thank you for your courtesy in speaking to me.'

Richard nodded, and the man scuttled off.

Half an hour ago, he had had no living relatives, and now it appeared he had four. He settled into the chair and put his boots on the stool.

The connection between himself and this parcel of ladies was so remote as to be almost nonexistent. They shared the same name and the same great-grandfather, but as far as he was concerned they were nothing to do with him. He would do what was necessary and continue with his life as before. He wasn't sure if he could actually refuse to take the title, but he certainly had no intention of being referred to as 'your grace'. He was a plain-speaking soldier and, although not a revolutionary, he had nothing but contempt for the officers from this background — the vast majority of which knew bugger all about soldiering, and had purchased their colours.

His lips twitched. He had purchased his; there was no other way to become an officer unless raised from the ranks, and that rarely happened. However, he had spent all his adult life in the military, and it suited him. He had no intention whatsoever of giving up his career in order to be the Duke of Denchester.

*December 1808, Suffolk, England*

Amanda believed that her mama had settled comfortably into their new abode, and even begun to approve of the move. There had been no further word from the lawyers about the arrival of the new duke, but at least they had been given further funds, which meant they could celebrate Christmastide in the old-fashioned way this year.

'Mama, my sisters and I are about to start making items to decorate the house for the festive period. Do you wish to participate?'

'My role is to approve, not to construct. I hate to admit it, my love, but I wish we had moved here earlier, as it is so much more comfortable. Would it be possible to invite a few friends for an informal supper party once the house is done?'

Beth clapped her hands. 'Shall we have a party? Will there be dancing? Can I attend?'

'Yes, sweetheart, we are to have a small gathering. If you can be prevailed upon to play the piano, dearest Amanda, then I do not see why the carpet could not be rolled back after supper.'

Beth ran across and flung her arms around their mother. 'I'm so happy we came here. Can I have a new gown? When will the party be?'

'You must ask your big sister, Beth, as I will leave all the details in her capable hands. Amanda, how many do you think we can accommodate in our new home?'

Sarah paced the length of the drawing room in order to settle this question. 'This is a generously sized chamber. If we move all the furniture to this end, I believe there would be room for a set to be formed. Perhaps as many as eight couples.'

'Then I shall begin to write a list. The weather is most unpleasant at present, but as soon as the rain stops you can send a footman to deliver the invitations.'

Amanda laughed — not something she had done much of recently. 'I think we had better establish a date for this event first, Mama. It's quite possible our neighbours are already committed, as it's already so close to the Lord's name day. I suggest the day before Christmas Eve would be perfect. Does everyone agree?'

There was a chorus of acceptance, and Beth skipped around the room. This gave them a little over two weeks to prepare. An informal supper party required as much planning as any other social event. Amanda had managed to avoid the torture of the obligatory London Season as she had taken a nasty tumble from her stallion and broken her leg. Although the injury had healed, she had been left with a slight limp; dancing, she believed, was now out of the question.

'Do I get a new gown, Amanda?' Beth asked plaintively.

'There's no time for any of us to have new gowns made, but between us I'm sure we can refurbish something we already have with fresh ribbons and lace.'

Her youngest sister pouted and stamped her foot. If something was not done to distract her, they would get a screaming tantrum. Darling Beth looked like a beautiful young lady on the outside, but was no more than six in her mind. She had been a perfectly normal little girl until she'd suffered from a near-fatal illness at that age, and had remained forever a small child.

'Come with me, Beth, and we'll examine the contents of all our wardrobes and see which gown will suit you best. I believe that Sarah has a delightful pink silk evening one that would be absolutely perfect for you.'

This was enough incentive for her sibling to clap her hands again. 'I'm coming, I'm coming! Sarah, you must come too.'

# 3

*December 1808, Corunna, Spain*

Richard didn't intend to inform his fellow officers that he had been quite unexpectedly elevated to the pinnacle of the aristocracy. The thought of being referred to as 'your grace' filled him with horror. He was plain Major Sinclair, and had no wish to be called anything else. There were several Lord This or Lord Thats in the army, but he knew few of them — they moved in a different circle to him.

He stared morosely into the fire. He had been a trifle curmudgeonly about helping the three young ladies and their mother, and regretted it now. He sincerely hoped the clerk wouldn't convey his exact words in the letter he was sending to them.

The principal estate was in Suffolk

— not a county he'd ever visited, but he thought it was the other side of Colchester. This was a town with a large barracks, and he'd had occasion to go there once or twice. He frowned. He'd need at least a sennight of leave in order to get there, do what was necessary, and return to London.

Most gentlemen would be wary of travelling country roads in winter, but after the horrendous march through Spain he'd just accomplished, to him it would be a mere bagatelle. He preferred to ride, but supposed he must arrive in style. No — he was damned if he would spend his blunt on a post-chaise or on buying a carriage and team. The common stage would be good enough for him. He had no manservant, travelled light, and would do perfectly well if he got a seat inside. It would necessitate at least one overnight stop, if not two, depending on the weather.

There was nothing further he could do until he reached England, and that was unlikely to be for another few weeks. The family had waited more than two years, so a couple more months would do them no harm.

\* \* \*

Eventually, he arrived in London in the middle of February. He was immediately given six weeks' leave of absence in order to put his affairs in order. The army wouldn't be returning to Spain until late spring, so as long as he reported for duty then, they were happy to let him go. After visiting the lawyers and confirming his identity, he was ready to depart. If they were dismayed by his dishevelled appearance, they hid it well. He was assured that there would be no delay in transferring everything to him.

'Riley, are you quite certain you wish to accompany me to the depths of Suffolk?'

'I am, sir. I got nothing better to do. I've been looking after you well enough these past few years and I ain't bothered if I'm called a servant and expected to behave subservient like.'

Richard had been obliged to take Riley into his confidence, but knew he could trust him to hold his tongue. 'Excellent. The stage leaves in an hour, which gives us barely sufficient time to get there. Our seats are reserved, but I doubt they'll be kept for us if we don't arrive at least one quarter of an hour before the vehicle departs.'

They arrived as the coach pulled into the inn yard. As both he and his companion were in regimentals, they were allowed to enter first — or maybe it was because the pair of them dwarfed the rest of the passengers.

As the weather was clement for the time of year, they were obliged to make only one stop, and that at Colchester at the Red Lion. They disembarked at Ipswich, and from there had to find their way to Denchester village, which he had discovered was no more than four miles' journey.

'We'll ride the remainder of the way, Riley. We need to purchase ourselves suitable horses. I wonder where we'll achieve our objective in this sleepy town.'

They had arrived at noon, and by mid-afternoon they were mounted on two massive beasts, well up to their weight, and more related to draught horses than hunters. As Richard intended to return to Corunna, he'd left his precious stallion at a livery stable to be taken care of in his absence.

Despite the workmanlike appearance of their steeds, they were strong and willing and covered the few miles in no time at all. He reined in at the massive iron gates to view what was ostensibly his own property. There was a gate-house, but it was unoccupied. The drive meandered into the distance and there was no sign of the house itself.

'Onward, Riley, let us see what awaits me. The woodland on either side of this drive is well-tended, and the drive appears to have no potholes. Apart from the lack of a gatekeeper, the dowager has not let the place deteriorate despite the lack of funds.'

'I reckon them that work for the estate are happy to work for naught, knowing all will be right and tight soon enough.'

It took them a further half an hour to be able to view Denchester Hall. He stared, lost for words.

'Is that yours, sir? It's as big as a palace.'

'It is indeed. It must take a small army of retainers to keep an edifice of this size in good heart. God knows what the annual wage bill is.' He clicked his tongue and his horse moved forward, eager to get into a warm stable. 'I'm in favour of employing as many as possible as long as there's blunt left over to help cover the expense of the war. The more souls working here, the fewer there are that will starve. The cost of war has pushed corn prices up too far.'

'Them villages we rode through were

likely in your demesne, and there were no signs of ill-repair. I reckon the few folk we saw were well fed and happy enough.'

Richard gestured towards the massive building. 'The shutters are closed, and it's not yet dark. There's no smoke from the chimneys. I think the family are not at home.'

'There'll be caretakers or suchlike. A place like this would not be left unoccupied or allowed to get damp.'

Richard was curious to know how his man knew so much about the ways of the toffs.

'My pa was head groom at a big house — not like this, mind, but a grand family they were.' Riley pointed to a track that led to the left of the drive. 'That will lead to the stables and such. No need to ride all the way to the big house what with no one being there.'

Two grooms appeared as they trotted into the immaculate yard. 'I am Major Sinclair. See to our mounts.'

The men bowed and rushed to attend to them. He dismounted, stiff and tired after many weeks of travelling. His attire was mired, he was unshaven, and his sergeant no better. All he wanted was a hot bath and something to eat. Tomorrow was soon enough to find the missing family.

*Suffolk, England*

Amanda was perusing a set of more satisfactory accounts when her siblings burst in. Beth ran over and grabbed her hand. 'Come with us, you must come at once. Two bad men have arrived at the Hall.'

She was on her feet in an instant. The staff had been given a leave of absence after working so hard to clean the entire building. Only a handful remained — those that had no relatives to visit.

'Sarah, did you see these intruders?'

'They were vagabonds, no doubt about it. They rode past as we were returning from our afternoon walk, and were unkempt and no gentlemen. They're both very large and spoke roughly.'

'Hmm . . . If they're riding rather than walking, they cannot be vagabonds, as they travel on foot.'

'The horses were huge, but very hairy, and not at all like your 'Thello,' Beth said. 'Are you coming to see?'

'I shall do so on my own. I must collect half a dozen stout men to accompany me in case there's fisticuffs. It would be better for you and our sister to remain here.'

At her suggestion there might be violence, both sisters nodded vigorously. 'You will be careful, won't you, Amanda? They looked very dangerous and fierce.'

She hugged Beth. 'Of course I will, sweetheart. Now, run along with Sarah to the nursery. I shall be back very soon to tell you all about it.'

Mama was visiting friends in the neighbourhood, thankfully, so would not have to be involved in this unpleasantness. She considered for a moment if she should request that the butler unlock the gun cupboard, but then decided against it.

Fortunately, there had been no rain for a week, and the ground underfoot was dry. She had snatched up her cloak and put her feet in her outdoor boots, but hadn't thought it necessary to find a bonnet. Ruffians wouldn't care either way if she was wearing one.

She could hear voices in the stable yard and increased her pace. The men who accompanied her were carrying cudgels, which she hoped would prove sufficient to persuade the unwanted visitors to leave. She stepped into the stable yard to accost them. They were about to take the path that led to the Hall, and she couldn't see their faces.

'You will leave these premises at once, or I shall have you removed by force. We do not want brigands like yourselves here. Take yourselves off at once.' She was pleased that her voice sounded authoritative and very loud. It certainly had the desired effect, as the man at the rear jumped as if stabbed in the derriere with a sharp object. He turned, and her mouth fell open. Who was the more surprised by the confrontation, it would have been to tell.

Facing her was the image of her father. Indeed, he could be her brother, so alike were they in features and colouring. Despite the fact that he was travel-worn and unshaved, she recognised immediately that he was the new Duke of Denchester.

Her knees were knocking as she dropped into a deep curtsy. 'I beg your pardon, your grace, I was misinformed. I am Lady Amanda Sinclair.'

'It is I who must beg your pardon, my lady. I thought the Hall to be empty, or would have come to the front door and announced myself.' He didn't sound at all put out by her less-than-friendly welcome.

She straightened and looked directly at him. He was staring equally hard at herself. His smile revealed a set of perfect teeth which seemed unnaturally white in his tanned face.

'We expected you last month, your grace. We moved to the Dower House in December, so you will have to reside with us until the staff return and the house can be reopened for you.'

'Then lead the way. This is my man, Riley; he is more a companion than a servant, and will require accommodation fitting to his status. I am Major Richard Sinclair, and he is my Sergeant-Major. I won't be referred to in any other way. Is that quite clear?'

'You are the head of the family — the Duke of Denchester — so you can hardly expect the staff to refer to you as 'Major Sinclair'. As you are a very distant cousin, then my mother, my sisters and I can refer to you as 'Cousin Richard'.'

His lips thinned and his eyes bored into hers. He wasn't pleased by her reply. But she refused to be browbeaten by a gentleman — if one could call him that at the moment — who had no idea how things were done in the aristocracy. She straightened her shoulders and glared right back.

Her intention had been to say something pithy, put him firmly in his place, but instead she said something else entirely. 'We could be siblings, Cousin Richard: you're the mirror image of my father. It will be pleasant not to be the only one with nut-brown curls and pale green eyes. Mama and my siblings have corn-coloured hair and bright blue eyes.'

His smile made him almost handsome, and heartbreakingly similar to the father she had loved and lost so recently. 'I own I was somewhat startled when I saw you. I thought to treat you as strangers, not relatives, but how can I do so when we're so alike?'

'You are our legal guardian, whether you like it or not. Follow me; the Dower House is a few hundred yards from here.'

In two strides he was beside her, and

his expression was no longer friendly. 'In which case, young lady, I suggest you desist from giving me orders. I hadn't intended to remain here long, but I'm beginning to suspect I'll not shake free of my responsibilities so easily.'

She was trying to breathe through her mouth, as the pungent odour wafting from him was enough to make her gag. Despite her efforts to hide her disgust, he laughed at her discomfort.

'I've been travelling for weeks, and not had the opportunity to bathe or change my raiment. I make no apologies for my disarray. I'm a military man through and through, and have no time for fops and those gentlemen that think more of their appearance than the well-being of others in their care.'

She moved away from him in the hope of breathing more easily, but his strides were long and he kept pace with her. There was no doubt he was doing it deliberately to aggravate her. One thing was certain: she must keep him away from her mother until he was more fragrant.

* * *

Richard was enjoying her discomfort. He certainly smelt rank — but who would not, in his circumstances? He did regret that at their first meeting he was so malodorous, and also that he had not brought more than a change of shirt and stockings.

No doubt there would be servants to sponge-clean and press his uniform, but what he was to wear until that was accomplished, he'd no notion. Taking pity on her, he dropped back in order to speak to Riley.

'The wretched girl is right. I can hardly expect the staff to ignore my elevation. In future, I suppose you must also refer to me as 'your grace'.'

'If you looks so like the old duke, maybe there's raiment of his that will fit you until you can get something made for you.'

47

He'd been about to deny the necessity of this, but then understood he was now trapped. He would have to resign his commission and allow Riley to return to duty. He would miss him. He was as much a friend as anything else.

'I must accept the inevitable. I shall give back my colours. Remain here until you're fully recovered from the journey, but then you must return to London and hand my resignation in for me.' He gripped his sergeant's arm. 'The worst of it is that I'll lose you. I've become accustomed to your presence these past years. I wish you could remain at my side in some capacity.'

Riley grinned. 'I reckon if you wants me, your grace, I'd be happy to stay. I've done me time, and was about to enlist for another five years.'

'Good God, man, that's the best news I've had in weeks. I'm like a fish out of water here, and will appreciate having you close by.'

'It were a rare sight to see you and

48

the lady side by side. You're like brother and sister. You'll fit in here no trouble. I wish I could say the same for me.'

'From now on you shall be my man of affairs. Don't look so apprehensive; no one will gainsay me. I've been leading my men for a decade. I hardly anticipate any difficulties running a household of women and servants.'

'If you'll give me leave, your grace, I'll go in the back way. Not fitting that I accompany you through the front.'

His man was carrying both bags, and he reached out to take his own. Riley shook his head. 'I'll act as your valet for now, sir, and get this lot pressed whilst you get cleaned up.'

'Get yourself a bath before you come to me. We both stink to high heaven, and we wouldn't want to cause offence with these fine ladies, now, would we?'

Amanda had hurried ahead and was almost out of sight. It was hardly dignified for a man in his position to run after her, but he did so anyway. He was fit, and covered the distance in seconds, arriving at her side before she reached the front steps. Her expression of distaste made the effort worthwhile. He was going to enjoy teasing her. It was far too long since he'd had any feminine company.

He stopped so suddenly his toes were crushed at the end of his boots. God's teeth! She was his ward, not someone he should flirt with. He'd no idea of her age, although he suspected the clerk had told him.

Once she was safely through the door he followed. He had half-expected to find the modest hallway filled with bowing servants, and was relieved to find it empty apart from a young footman.

'If you would care to come with me, your grace, your apartment has been made ready for you, and everything you require is waiting.'

Richard looked from side to side as he ascended the staircase. Everywhere he looked, he saw replicas of himself. It was quite extraordinary how the unusual colouring had passed down through the generations on both sides of the family tree.

He was ushered ceremoniously into a comfortable sitting room, and from there to a decent bedchamber which also had a dressing room. In here had been set out a hip bath, and the lemon-scented water steamed invitingly. There was also a smaller tub, which was exactly what he wanted.

Ignoring the young man, he stripped off, but did not step in. He was handed a cloth and a bar of sweet-smelling soap. He scrubbed himself from head to foot, rinsing the grime off in the smaller tub as he did so. When he was certain he was clean, he lowered himself into the hip bath.

For a large man like himself, only his backside and torso could fit in — his legs and feet were obliged to remain on the floor in front. The first thing he would do would be to have one of those newfangled bathing rooms installed. He'd heard tell that there was a bathing tub made that could accommodate one's entire length. Being able to be fully immersed in hot water would almost be worth the inconvenience of being a duke.

# 4

'Amanda, I can hardly credit that those disreputable gentlemen are in fact the duke and his manservant. Are you quite sure he's not an impostor?' Sarah asked.

'I'm absolutely certain. He has no need to produce any papers, as I accept wholeheartedly that he is the gentleman we've been waiting for these past two years. When you see him, you will know how I came so quickly to this decision.' Amanda had no intention of telling her sister that Cousin Richard was the image of their departed father. She wanted to see her face when they were introduced.

'He has no luggage; how can he dress for dinner without it? Do you think it will arrive separately?'

'He has been a soldier all his life. I doubt that he has anything apart from his regimentals to wear. I intend to send a letter by express to Weston's in Town, instructing them to visit immediately and set in hand his new wardrobe.'

'But the other person — he is so large and so rough-looking.'

'He is a sergeant-major, so must be an able soldier. I'm certain he will appear less alarming once he's clean-shaven.'

Her sister sighed. 'I'd always imagined that officers were handsome, romantic gentlemen, but our new Cousin Richard is neither.'

She looked away, hurt by the remark. If her dearest sister considered Richard unattractive, then she must believe the same to have been true for their dear departed papa and herself, as they were of identical looks and colouring.

'Mind you,' Sarah continued, unaware that her thoughtless words had cut deep, 'I didn't really see their faces, so am being rather premature in my judgement. They are both very large gentlemen, which is a good thing. I cannot abide a short man, can you?'

Amanda smiled, relieved that she had — not for the first time — jumped to the wrong conclusion. She was oversensitive about her lack of looks in comparison to the rest of her family, and felt she must try harder not to be so silly. Having such lovely sisters was, however, a constant reminder of what she lacked.

'For me, it would mean looking at the top of his head. I must write that letter and get it taken to the village right away.'

As she was hurrying to the study to complete this task, another thing occurred to her. She spoke to one of the footmen and set it in motion before continuing. How long would it take her new cousin to complete his ablutions? Papa had been somewhat careless of his appearance, much to her mother's annoyance, and rarely spent more than half an hour with his valet.

The door to the study was open, so

that when she rang the little brass bell on her desk it could be heard quite clearly as far away as the entrance hall. She must send a message to her mother, informing her that the wait was over and that their fortunes were restored. No doubt the new duke would wish to reside in his ancestral home, but she was determined that they would remain where they were, as it was so much more manageable and far more comfortable than the vast, draughty, old-fashioned Hall.

Once the necessary letters were written and dispatched, she went in search of her younger sister. She hoped Beth hadn't been too upset by the encounter with what she had thought were unwanted intruders.

'Beth, has your sister come up to the nursery to speak to you?'

'She has, Amanda. Does that mean we have to move back to that horrible old Hall? I like it here so much better.'

'As do I, sweetheart. As far as I'm concerned, Cousin Richard must move to the Hall, and we shall remain here in comfort.'

Nanny, who looked after the needs of her youngest sibling, nodded happily. 'I'm relieved to hear you say so, my lady; it's ever so warm and pleasant here. Lady Beth has been more settled in this nursery than she ever was at the Hall.'

Amanda moved away from her sister so she could not be overheard, and the elderly lady, who had been in the family for decades, followed her.

'Nanny, I would like you to keep Beth up here for the moment. Until I have explained the circumstances to his grace, I have no wish for there to be any misunderstandings.'

'Lady Sarah will wish to have her come-out now — does that mean you'll be opening up the London house? It might be easier for Lady Beth to remain here with me.'

'I haven't given the matter any thought, but now that you mention it, we can hardly delay her debut any

57

longer. Lady Sarah will be overjoyed to spend a few months in Town, but I'll remain here.'

They parted in full agreement. There was no suggestion that she should accompany Sarah. A plain young lady with a limp, however rich and well-bred, would not be sought after by the entitled aristocrats looking for a suitable bride. Her role was to take care of her little sister, who would never be able to have a home or family of her own.

Her duties attended to for the moment, she was in sore need of some fresh air. She paused long enough to snatch up her cloak, and made her way through the house and out into the garden. The sun was still out, although there was no warmth in it at this time of year, and there were daffodils and snowdrops to be admired.

★　★　★

When the water got cold, Richard stepped out of the bath and enveloped himself in a large bath sheet. Then, still dripping, he walked into his bedchamber. The fire was roaring in the grate, the room unpleasantly hot. After years in the army, he had no time for overheated rooms, and much preferred the windows open however cold it was outside.

He strode to the windows, determined to fling them open. The house was of relatively modern construction, probably built in the last fifty years, unlike the Hall which had been around for centuries and was in dire need of modernisation.

The first window moved up smoothly, letting in a welcome blast of fresh air. The second proved more recalcitrant, and in his struggle to push it open, the towel around his hips slithered to the floor. Unbothered by this inconvenience, he heaved, and the damned thing shot up so fast only his quick reactions saved him from tumbling headfirst through it. His loud expletives echoed around the garden.

As he pushed himself back to safety, he looked up. To his horror, he saw Amanda staring at him, open-mouthed. He bowed, and to his amusement she fled. He stepped back so he was no longer visible, still laughing.

'Your grace, Lady Amanda thought that these garments might be of use to you until you have others of your own.' The young man who was acting as his temporary valet pointed to an array of jackets, shirts and breeches spread out on the bed. He was about to refuse, but something made him investigate further. He was taller and broader in the shoulders than most men. He was curious to know why the girl had thought these would be of any use to him.

'To whom did they belong?' he addressed the young man, who had had the sense not to offer him the towel to cover his nakedness.

'Forgive me for saying so, your grace, but you are the very image of the last duke. These were his garments. Lady

Amanda had them stored in the attic at the Hall, and sent for them immediately you arrived.'

'Before I attempt to try them, I need a shave. Also, cut my hair to a more suitable length.'

This time he wrapped the towel back around his middle before he took his seat in front of the washstand. He preferred to shave himself, and wondered how the young man would cope — but he performed well.

Richard stared into the glass, scarcely recognising himself. He no longer looked like a vagabond — could almost be mistaken for a gentleman. The shorter hairstyle suited him, and he decided he would keep it this way in future.

He wasn't sure if he was annoyed or pleased by Amanda's interference in his affairs. There was nothing in the pile of clothes to offend his simple tastes. 'I've no interest in sartorial matters; I'll leave you to select whatever you think will do.'

The shirt he was handed fitted him perfectly. The stockings were equally comfortable. He pulled on the unmentionables, and they too were ideal. This was extraordinary indeed — not only did he have the colouring of his predecessor, but it appeared he also had the same physical build.

He was unsurprised that the dark blue jacket was a perfect fit. He suffered the annoyance of having his valet tie his stock.

'Is there anything else you would like me to do for you, your grace?'

'What's your name?'

'James, your grace, at your service.'

'Then you shall retain the position as my valet. Do you have something other than your footman's uniform to wear?'

'I do, your grace. Thank you. I'll not let you down.' The young man backed away as if leaving the presence of royalty, but Richard beckoned him back.

'James, I stand on no ceremony. I might now hold the title of the Duke of

Denchester, but I'm still a military man at heart. There's no need to bow and scrape you can call me *sir*, not *your grace*, when we're in private. Wherever you are lodging at present, I need you close to me.'

'I understand, sir, and will have my things moved to the boxroom across the hall.' He smiled tentatively, as if not sure such a thing was acceptable. 'If you open the door and shout, I'll hear you well enough, sir.'

'Excellent. I can see that we're going to get along famously. Will I do? I've no wish to scare the ladies a second time.'

'You look every inch a duke, sir, if you don't mind my saying so.'

Richard slapped him on the back as he strolled past. He rather thought he not only looked the part, but might well be mistaken for the son of the deceased, rather than a distant relative. It was a strange feeling to be a part of a family when for most of his life he'd been on his own.

Before he went downstairs, he thought

he would explore the house, as this was to be his home for the foreseeable future. There was no way on earth he was going to move into that huge place until it had been modernised. Perhaps it would be less expensive to raze it to the ground rather than tinker about trying to bring it up to scratch.

There was a dozen or more doors on this floor, so there must be more than enough bedchambers for everybody even if he remained on the premises. He had no intention of opening any of them, so instead took the staircase that led to the second floor, where he assumed the nursery and schoolroom would be situated.

He frowned — would the Dower House have such things? This must have been built to house the dowager of some past duke, which would mean that there would have been no necessity to provide chambers for children. It was more likely these rooms were for upper servants. He was about to turn back when he heard a young lady laughing, and decided to investigate.

He stepped into a wide corridor which ran the width of the house. Light flooded in from the windows at both ends, making it a pleasant place to be. There was evidence that these were indeed rooms for children and their retainers. There was a magnificent rocking horse, and also an impressive dolls' house.

The door from which the laughing had come was open. A beautiful young lady dashed out and skidded to a halt upon seeing him. Her eyes rounded and her hands flew to her mouth.

'I beg your pardon, my lady. I'm the new duke — call me Cousin Richard.'

An elderly lady in white apron and mob cap appeared beside her. She curtsied deeply. 'Your grace, this is Lady Elizabeth. She is the youngest daughter of the previous duke.'

The girl recovered her composure and made an awkward curtsy. Her smile was tentative, but she seemed less apprehensive now. 'You look just like my papa. Your hair's the same colour as my sister Amanda's. I have hair like my mama and my other sister, Sarah.'

It all became clear to him now. This beautiful girl was intellectually impaired, which was why she resided on the nursery floor. 'I am wearing his clothes too. Do you think your mama will mind?'

She giggled and shook her head, her golden ringlets bouncing. 'She will tell you to get your own clothes, Cousin Richard. She didn't like my papa very much. Will you come and see my drawings?'

'I should love to, sweetheart, thank you for inviting me.'

He spent a delightful hour with her, and left promising to return later in the day. It broke his heart to see her so impaired. She might have the mind of a small child, but had the appearance of a lovely young woman. This made her vulnerable to predators.

He vowed then to take care of her, to make sure that her life remained happy and unsullied by unpleasantness from unscrupulous gentlemen looking for an heiress. He strolled downstairs, having quite forgotten the amusing incident at the window that had taken place earlier.

★　★　★

Amanda was still shaking when she burst into the house through the side door. Her cheeks were hot, her throat clogged with tears. How could he stand there and bow? She had never seen even the naked chest of a gentleman, and now she had seen everything.

A further wave of heat spread from her toes to her crown. How could she face him ever again after what had happened? She was quite sure that even a married woman was never treated to such a spectacle. If only she hadn't been there when it had happened. She could never unsee that moment.

Slowly, her heart returned to its normal beat, and her legs stopped trembling. Where could she go to find peace and privacy? The study — nobody came there to disturb her without an invitation. The estate manager took care of the day-to-day matters, but it was her responsibility to run the household and manage the finances. Mama had insisted she could no longer do so after Papa died.

Once inside she closed the door and wanted, for the first time, a lock on it. She collapsed into the chair in front of the fire and closed her eyes. Having seen countless men and gentlemen fully clothed, and the male anatomy of her stallion and the half-dozen dogs that roamed about the place, she could not for the life of her understand why seeing him as nature intended had shaken her to the very core.

Cousin Richard, even from that distance, had been clearly tanned from the sun. His shoulders were wide, his arms muscular, the column of his neck strong. She had not seen much of his legs, but she imagined they too were well-rounded and sturdy. She pushed the image of the part of his body that came between his chest and his legs out of her head. She hoped never to see such a sight again in her entire life.

Then her lips quivered. She had no intention of becoming a bride because she must look after her sister and her mother. Even if she desired to be a wife, it was unlikely that someone bracket-faced and with a limp would attract a partner. She now had the advantage over every other unmarried lady. She knew exactly what an unclothed male body looked like — and she sincerely wished she didn't.

Too restless to settle to any sensible task, she paced the room trying to get her thoughts in order. If Mama ever heard about the incident, she shuddered to think what would be the outcome. If merely being in the same room alone with a gentleman meant that both parties were compromised, heaven knew what society would consider the correct procedure after what had transpired between herself and this man.

Would he feel obligated to make her an offer? Did he think that she had engineered the whole thing in order to trap him into unwanted matrimony? One thing she did know was that she could never marry a man who had killed for his living; so, even if he made her an offer, she would immediately refuse. Fiddlesticks to that! She was getting carried away with her imaginings. After all, it was hardly her fault he chose to appear at the window completely without clothes at the very moment she was walking past.

A curious thought stopped her in her tracks. Perhaps the boot was on the other foot — had he done this deliberately in order to force her into accepting his hand? No, the very idea was ludicrous. He had become, by his elevation, the most eligible bachelor in the kingdom. He could have his pick of the young ladies on the marriage mart, and certainly wouldn't be interested in a flawed specimen such as herself.

What had transpired was unfortunate and embarrassing for both of them but, in her opinion, there was no need to make too much of it. As far as she was concerned, she would treat him as she had before and pretend nothing untoward had taken place in the garden an hour ago.

As the housekeeper had already been advised to prepare a more elaborate dinner tonight, there was nothing left for Amanda to do. She wouldn't lurk in the study a moment longer, but repair to the drawing room. When he came down he would find her calm and relaxed and reading the latest novel that had arrived from Hatchards only yesterday.

Sarah was already there, and jumped to her feet at Amanda's appearance. 'He will be down in a moment, so I'm informed, and I cannot wait to meet him.'

'I consider him part of the family already, and I'm certain that you will too once you've seen him.'

A slight sound at her back warned her that he was there. Instead of turning around, she spoke with her back to him. The longer she could avoid looking him in the eye, the better. 'Cousin Richard, I should be grateful if you desisted from creeping about the place. It's enough to give a person palpitations.'

His rich baritone laugh sounded from directly behind her, making her take an involuntary step forward. 'I most humbly beg your pardon, Amanda. I shall endeavour to make as much noise as possible in future.'

He stepped around her and moved smoothly to her sister. 'You must be Sarah. You and Beth could be twins. I am delighted to make your acquaintance.' He bowed and her sister curtsied.

'We are pleased that you've arrived at last, Cousin Richard, as long as you don't require us to transfer back to the Hall. It's far more comfortable here.'

'We shall all remain where we are whilst I decide what to do with that monstrosity. I'm considering flattening it and building again. Something smaller, more convenient to live in and to run.'

'That house has been the ancestral home of the Sinclairs for hundreds of years. How can you make such a decision when you've been here less than a day?' Amanda was so incensed at his casual dismissal of the Denchester family seat, she quite forgot that she actually agreed with him.

# 5

Richard understood Amanda's dismay. In her shoes he would feel exactly the same. 'I've no intention of beginning any demolition or major alterations without discussing it with you and your mother first.' Even as he spoke these words, he understood that it was his right to do as he pleased and for her to do as she was told. He looked at the fierce young lady in front of him. Her eyes, exactly like his own, sparkled like gemstones. An attractive flush stained her cheeks, making her look almost pretty.

'My dear girl, we mustn't be at daggers drawn so early in our acquaintance. As you so rightly pointed out earlier, we could be siblings. You and your sisters are my responsibility. I give you my word that I've no intention of being a demanding guardian.'

Her smile was reward enough. 'Then I thank you, cousin, and welcome you to the family. You said that you met my youngest sister . . .'

He nodded. 'She's in need of my protection more than you or Sarah. I can assure you that I'll keep her safe.'

'We love her dearly, but are well aware that although in her mind she'll not become an adult, in body she will, and that's where the danger lies.'

The other girl moved trustingly towards him and stared earnestly up at him. 'Am I to have my debut in Town this year? I shall be nineteen years of age in the summer, and be considered almost at my last prayers if I leave it much longer.'

'If your mother is willing to make the arrangements then I've no objection. However, I have far too much to do here to accompany you.'

'Mama will expect you to lead me out at my ball, but I'm sure if you depart after that it will be acceptable.' She smiled confidingly. 'Our mother

75

has no head for organisation, and will be more interested in playing cards than scrutinising my partners. She relies entirely on Amanda to do the things that matter in the household.'

He was about to refuse when Amanda stepped in. 'Cousin Richard, if you're not there, my sister might well be taken advantage of by some unscrupulous fortune-hunter. It would be unconscionable for you to abandon her to her own devices.'

'You will be there to take care of that sort of thing . . .'

'Oh, but I shall not. I never travel. Beth relies on me at all times, and would be bereft if I was not there. You realise, of course, that she cannot go to London herself.'

'If I go, my dear, then you shall go too, and so shall Beth. I'm sure she'll enjoy seeing the menagerie, driving around Green Park and promenading in Bond Street. When does the Season start?'

'Members of the *ton* will start

arriving in London next month. I have no wish to accompany you, but will do so if you agree to escort my sister and ensure she's not pestered by the wrong sort of gentleman.'

Sarah joined in the conversation. 'If I'm to have a ball, then invitations must be sent out by the end of this month, or all the best dates will be taken by other people. Do you have any idea of to whom we should send one?'

'Are you addressing me or your sister? I know nothing about such matters. I'm sure that Amanda and your mother will have things in place in time.'

'Have you never attended a ball, Cousin Richard?'

'As an army officer, I was obliged to do so. I can also dance if forced to, but it's not something I enjoy.'

'I've never danced with a gentleman,' Sarah said. 'If my sister plays for us, will you dance with me after dinner so that I might practise my steps?' The girl — for she was little more than that to him — turned to Amanda pleadingly.

'I'd be happy to, as long as I'm not expected to practice *my* steps,' Amanda replied. 'I'll sit with the other chaperones at the edge of the ballroom. You do realise that you cannot waltz — only married ladies are allowed to do so.'

This statement intrigued him. 'Who is the arbitrator of this decision? Surely a young lady at her own ball can do as she pleases?'

'She can indeed, but if she does so, her reputation will be gone. Society has rigid rules, Cousin Richard, and they must be adhered to at all times. My sister knows how to deport herself in company.' She sighed theatrically. 'I suppose I must set about writing letters to London in order to have the house opened in Grosvenor Square. The staff employed at the Hall will be returning from their leave at the end of the week, and they can transfer to our town house.'

'How big is that place?'

'Not as big as the Hall, but it has more than two dozen bedchambers, most of which have their own sitting rooms and dressing rooms. It also has a beautiful garden at the rear of the building, and coach houses and stabling for dozens of horses.'

'Then we take our own cattle with us. If we overnight twice at suitable hostelries, I'm sure the horses will complete the journey without difficulty.'

Sarah saw the carriage containing their mother turn into the drive, and rushed to greet her and give her the good news. Amanda turned to him.

'We will all need a new wardrobe, and this must be set in motion at once. Fortunately, there's no necessity to send away for material or seamstresses, as we have our own. Mama has accumulated a vast stock of materials and the necessary threads, ribbons, buttons and beads to make up any number of gowns.'

'I'm no expert, but even so I can see that you and your sisters are dressed in the height of fashion. By the way, I take it that it is you I have to thank for the loan of your father's clothes.'

'I wasn't sure if you'd be offended. It's uncanny how alike you are. No doubt you wish to view your new home before you demolish it, and I'll show you the portraits of our ancestors. You are the image of every one of them.'

'I should like that. Meanwhile, I need to purchase some decent horseflesh for myself and Riley before we leave. The nags we came on were all that was available at short notice.'

Her eyes narrowed and she looked him up and down. 'You may have the use of my stallion, Othello, until you find something suitable. He's more than up to your weight.'

For some inexplicable reason she didn't wait to hear his thanks: her cheeks flushed, and she rushed off. What the devil was wrong with the girl?

★ ★ ★

Amanda escaped for the second time that day to the sanctuary of the study

80

before remembering that her mother had returned and would expect her to introduce him. She flapped a periodical up and down in front of her overheated face. It had been a disastrous error of judgement to look at him so closely especially at his nether regions.

She recovered her equilibrium and made her way back to the entrance hall — not a moment too soon, as Mama burst in, eager to meet the new arrival. He was standing with his back to the door, gazing pensively out of the window at the far end of the room. The less she saw of his front, the better, as far as she was concerned.

'Introduce me at once, Amanda. Sarah says he's to take us to Town, so that she will make her come out this year after all.'

'That's correct. He's in the drawing room.'

Her mother rushed ahead, not giving her time to say anything about his extraordinary likeness to the departed duke, or the fact that he was dressed in Papa's garments.

'Dear boy, I cannot tell you how relieved I am that you have arrived at last. It has been a misery . . . '

He turned. Her mother gasped, and crumpled senseless to the carpet.

For a second, Amanda was frozen to the spot — but not him. He was instantly on his knees beside her and running his hands along her limbs to check for damage.

'God damn it to hell! That was clumsy of me — and of you, Amanda,' he said as he scooped her mother from the carpet and gently placed her on the *chaise longue*. 'Didn't it occur to you to warn her that not only do I look like your father, but am also dressed in his clothes?'

Mama was coming round, and colour was returning to her cheeks. 'I intended to do so, but wasn't given the opportunity. I think she would be more shocked at your language, sir, than your appearance if she had heard it. I hope never to hear such words in this house again.'

He ignored her remark and turned his attention to the patient. 'Your grace, I apologise for startling you. My similarity to your husband must have been a dreadful shock, especially as I'm wearing his raiment.'

'I forgive you, Richard; you cannot be blamed for your appearance. I take it that your luggage has been delayed?'

'Worse than that, ma'am, I have no luggage. If you have no objection, I'll continue to make use of your husband's wardrobe until I can replace them.'

'I've already sent a letter by express to Weston's, cousin, and somebody should come tomorrow or the next day with samples.'

Why did this information seem to prove less than welcome? One would have thought that a person in his position would be grateful for all the assistance offered. She ignored his fulminating stare and turned her attention to her mother.

'Mama, are you better? Do you wish me to organise the opening of our town house?'

'Yes, do so at once. I shall begin to draw up a list of the families who must be invited to Sarah's ball. I do wish you had not given my companion leave to visit her ailing mother — when is she expected to return?'

'Not until after the funeral.'

'I had forgotten that detail. Far better the poor woman died than lingered on for weeks and deprived me of Miss Bennett's assistance for even longer. Now, I am recovered.' She smiled at him, quite unaware that her callous statement had offended all of them. 'We dress for dinner.'

'That is your prerogative, ma'am, but I have no intention of doing so. Evening dress, as far as I'm concerned, is worn only when there are guests.' He nodded and strode out, his back rigid with disapproval.

'What a strange young man he is, I declare. Run along and write the necessary letters, Amanda, whilst your sister and I go to the sewing room in order to peruse the fashion plates and set in motion the new gowns we shall need.'

'Mama, Cousin Richard insists that we all go to London, not just you and Sarah.'

'Then I suppose that you have no option but to accompany us. I expect Beth would have felt left out if we hadn't included her in this venture. She cannot attend public functions, but with you beside her, I think she could come to any event we hold in our own home.'

'Not to anything so grand as a ball, but something similar to the event we held last December would be ideal. I must write my letters first, but will join you upstairs immediately afterwards. I'm certain it will take you and Sarah far longer to choose gowns than it will take me to deal with my correspondence.'

With the letters sent off to be

delivered in the next mailbag, Amanda made her way to the small apartment that had been designated as the sewing room. It was in fact a minor guestroom and had a bedchamber plus a small parlour. The bolts of material and other necessities were stored in what had been the bedroom, and the sitting room was where the work was done.

'There you are, my dear; we have just completed our selections. Do you wish my assistance to choose? I am perfectly content to remain here and offer my opinion — or shall I leave you and Sarah to make the decisions without my interference?'

Mama was a contradiction. One moment she was insensitive, and the next quite the opposite. 'You know I've not your expertise in such matters. I should be grateful of your assistance — please stay.'

After an exhausting hour, the selection had been made, and she was finally free to go about her business. If Cousin Richard wasn't about to change into evening clothes, then neither would she.

Amanda waited until her mother had departed in a flurry of silk and petticoats. 'Sarah, I don't intend to change — I think it might be wise if you do. I've no wish for Mama to feel isolated by being the only person at dinner in an elaborate ensemble.'

'Shouldn't we follow his lead? After all, he's now our guardian and head of the household.'

'I cannot dispute that fact, but he's ignorant of the ways of *ton*. By his own admission he is a military man and knows no other life but that of soldiering. It's he that should follow our lead, not the other way around.'

Her sister giggled at the suggestion. 'I think that highly unlikely, don't you? He will do things his own way regardless of etiquette, fashion, or the dictates of society. He is a duke and can do as he pleases, I fear we cannot do the same.'

'It's certainly going to be an interesting few weeks, my love. Are you quite certain you wish to go in search of a husband? I'd hoped to have you around for year or two longer.'

'Good grief — I don't intend to become betrothed. I want at least three Seasons before I make a decision of that sort. I know you don't like dancing, parties, or anything of that sort, but I do. I cannot wait to be whirling around the dance floor in the arms of a handsome gentleman.'

'Which reminds me, I'd better look through my music and find something suitable for you to practise your steps after dinner tonight.'

★ ★ ★

Richard had recovered his temper by the time he reached the side door. He decided to go and examine the horse Amanda had so generously offered him the use of. He was damned if he knew why a young lady, however proficient she was on horseback, would have a stallion as her hack.

The grooms bowed low when he arrived, and he nodded in acknowledgement. The stable block was as immaculate as the yard, and he was confident the animals residing here would be well taken care of. There was no need for him to ask the whereabouts of the stallion, as a huge black horse, ears pricked, held pride of place in the first double-sized stall.

'Well, Othello, I see why you are so named.' He pulled the silky ears and was slobbered over for his trouble. This animal might be a stallion, but he was soft as butter, and he understood immediately why Amanda had him as her own.

'Excuse me, your grace; I'm Sydney, head groom. Is there anything you wish to know about the horses here?'

'I have left my own beast in Corunna as I thought to be returning there. Is there someone here you would trust to fetch him for me?'

'There is indeed, your grace. Thomas, under-groom here, would be ideal. The old duke always sent him all over the country to deliver and collect horses. He once went to Ireland to purchase two mares to add to his stud.'

This was news indeed. 'Is there a stud farm on the estate?'

'There is indeed, sir, and it's continued to flourish these past two years. We have two stallions at stud, and half a dozen mares. Lady Amanda takes a keen interest in this venture, and used to accompany his grace to horse sales and race meetings.'

'As Lady Amanda suggested I ride her horse, then I take it there's nothing suitable available for me at present?'

'Not at all, your grace — I can think of two geldings that would be perfect. They are both spoken for, but in the circumstances I'm sure Sir Jonathan Fitzpatrick and Squire Bottomley would be happy to relinquish their claims.'

'Is the stud farm far from here?'

'Two miles. I'll have Othello saddled

for you at once. Do you wish someone to accompany you?'

'Give me directions and I'll find it myself.'

The stallion, despite his apparently meek nature, was a lively ride, and Richard enjoyed every minute of the journey to the farm. He viewed the two animals and they were indeed exactly what he wanted. He cantered back into the yard well-satisfied with his visit.

As he dismounted, the stable clock struck five. He was tardy. Despite his determination not to change his clothes to dine, he could hardly appear smelling of the stables. Either way — he was going to cause offence.

He hurtled up the backstairs and into his apartment.

'Your hot water is waiting, your grace, and a fresh outfit. If you allow me to remove your boots, I can polish them whilst you wash.' His new valet was a marvel — even better than Riley.

In less than a quarter of an hour he was clean, freshly garbed and his boots were shining. As he took the stairs two at a time, he wondered why James had not set out evening wear. Was he clairvoyant, or had his brusque comments about changing for dinner been overheard and repeated below stairs?

He slowed his pace before entering the drawing room, his breathing as even as if he hadn't run. The three ladies weren't pacing the floor looking irritated at his tardiness, but were conversing happily in front of the fire.

'Good evening, your grace, Amanda, Sarah. I do hope I've not kept you waiting long.'

The duchess was resplendent in a puce silk evening gown with matching feathers in her hair. Sarah had on a simpler ensemble, a pale blue gown which suited her fair colouring to perfection. However, Amanda was wearing the same outfit as earlier.

'Not at all, young man; dinner has yet to be announced.' She gestured towards his jacket and pulled a face. 'I cannot see why you object putting on evening rig, but are quite prepared to put on a fresh jacket and breeches.'

He was about to explain but Amanda forestalled him. She rose gracefully to her feet and smiled warmly. 'I fear I'm the only one not to have changed into something different. I take it your visit to the stud went well?'

'Thank you for enquiring. I can see why you're so attached to your stallion. I thoroughly enjoyed our ride, but am not taking him from you as I now have the two geldings your head groom recommended.'

The butler appeared at the door and they followed him to the dining room.

# 6

Richard had expected to be served numerous courses and removes all smothered with rich cream sauces but the reverse was true. The food was well-cooked, simple and delicious. He couldn't remember having eaten so well for many years.

'Does Beth not eat with us?'

'She prefers nursery tea, cousin, but always joins us for breakfast and luncheon.' Beth found elaborate meals and rich food not to her taste. 'It was kind of you to spend time with her upstairs, and she seems very taken with you.'

'And I with her. Though she has the face and figure of a lovely young woman, yet the mind of a child — a dangerous combination. I intend to appoint a companion for her before we leave. I don't wish you to be burdened

94

with her care, Amanda. You should have the opportunity to attend as many social functions as you wish.'

'My daughter prefers to remain in the background, young man! She'll not attend any soirées, routs, or balls unless you drag her there. She believes her limp means she must remain forever a wallflower.'

'Absolute balderdash! Your limp's imperceptible, Amanda, and you've yet to reach your majority. I insist that you attend as many functions as your sister.' Her eyes flashed, but he continued before she could speak. 'If I'm obliged to skip about like a nincompoop, then you must suffer with me. We shall stand up together, and then glower at the others enjoying themselves.'

Unwillingly, her lips curved. 'As you put it so persuasively, sir, I can hardly refuse. You must dance with my sister as well before you're allowed to glower at the edge of the ballroom with me.' Her smile was quite delightful as she continued, 'I shall be one-and-twenty in

July, so I'm almost there.'

After the meal had ended, he pretended he didn't know it was customary for the lady of the house to rise and take the other women with her whilst the gentleman remained to drink port. He tossed his napkin aside and stood up.

'I promise to dance with you, Sarah, if your sister will play. Let's get it over with so we can enjoy the remainder of the evening in peace.' He smiled at the duchess. 'Do you play cards, your grace?'

She was on her feet in an instant. 'There's nothing I like better, sir. We shall play a few hands of Loo, or Whist if you prefer. Hurry up, girls, let us get this dancing nonsense out of the way so we can sit down like sensible adults at the card table.'

The piano was at the far end of the drawing room, and Amanda made her way to it immediately. It took two footmen only a few minutes to roll up the carpet and move it to one side where no one could fall over it. Richard was unsurprised that the boards underneath it were as polished and clean as the area around the edges of the room.

Amanda began to play a lively tune. Richard led his younger cousin through a series of intricate steps, and was impressed by her lightness of foot and natural rhythm. She would make any gentleman a perfect partner. Although not quite as intelligent as her older sister, she wasn't a dull girl. After half a dozen dances were performed, he led her to the edge of the floor.

'Do you play? I'd like to dance with your sister now, if possible.'

Sarah nodded happily. 'Not as well as she does, but well enough for the purpose. Did you hear that?' she called across the room. 'Cousin Richard is going to dance with you now, and I'm going to play for you both.'

He gave Amanda no option, but took her hand and refused to release it. Unless she struggled, she had no recourse but to follow him onto the temporary dance floor.

'I'm a very indifferent partner, your grace, and I would have thought you'd had enough of dancing after spending so long with my sister.'

'Not at all.' He tucked her arm through his and guided her to the far end of the room, where they could not be overheard, whilst Sarah searched through the music for something she could play easily.

'I'm a military man, as I told you before, and not some jackanapes who's done nothing more energetic than ride to hounds or do a few rounds in a boxing parlour. I can march with my men for miles if necessary, then fight a battle, and repeat the process the following day with no sleep and little to eat.'

God knew why he'd told her this — it was hardly a suitable subject for a delicately bred young lady. To his surprise and delight, she stopped pulling against him and spun to face him.

'You will be the first duke in this family to have had any life outside the aristocracy. Your children will add strength to the line. I sincerely hope that your ability as an officer will transfer to the more mundane role of running the estate.'

★　★　★

His reaction to her outrageous mention of his ability to father healthy children was everything it should be. His smile made her miss her step, but his arm around her waist held her upright.

'Sarah, can you play a waltz?' His voice carried wonderfully well down the length of the drawing room.

'I have the music for one here, cousin, and shall play it for you.'

Shouting back and forth in front of their parent was unheard of, but she was given no opportunity to observe mama's reaction to such scandalous behaviour as she was swept away by him. She scarcely knew the steps but that was immaterial as he guided her skilfully throughout.

Being whirled around the dance floor in this way was an experience she'd never thought to have, and quite changed her mind about the pleasure of dancing. When the final notes faded, she was breathless and it wasn't all related to the exercise.

He smiled down at her. 'Well, cousin, I should say that your ability to dance is no longer in question. I don't give a damn what the tabbies say: I intend to waltz with you at every opportunity.'

She stepped away and curtsied, and he bowed as if they were indeed at a grand ball. 'I thank you, your grace, for the dance. It was most enjoyable. A once-in-a-lifetime experience.' She thought this made it quite plain that she'd no intention of doing anything so silly as performing this risque dance with him in public. He was about to reply when she continued, 'I must ask you for a second time to refrain from using immoderate language in my presence.'

Instead of being offended by her reprimand, he laughed. 'I've told you more than once, my dear, that I'm a rough soldier who just happens to be a duke. In my experience, someone as high in the instep as myself can do as he damn well pleases, and no one will raise an eyebrow.' He reached out and pushed a stray curl from her cheek. 'I can see there are advantages to this position after all.'

She was left confused, not sure if he was referring to the pleasure of being acquainted with her, or the fact that he believed he was able to swear whenever he pleased without consideration of one's feelings on the subject.

Her mother was becoming impatient at the delay. 'That is quite enough dancing for tonight. I am waiting to begin a hand of cards.'

Amanda exchanged a smile with her partner, and then the three of them hurried to the card table.

The next few days were filled with fittings, list writing, and general upheaval as she planned for the exodus of the entire staff and themselves to Town for the Season. They would be away from the end of March until the end of May — not that long, really — but it required meticulous planning.

Amanda had run the household in her mother's stead for the past two years, as her parent had been devastated by Papa's passing and unable to function normally for the first few months. Having handed over the troublesome business of being the lady of the house, Mama had been reluctant to take it back. Reluctance must be a flaw in the Sinclair family, as Richard — she refused to add the appendage *cousin* to his name any longer — had also proved reluctant to take up his duties.

That said, she couldn't fault his dedication now that he was actually

102

here. He had been tramping about the Hall most days, and then ousted her from the study so that he could use it for his own business. She wasn't best pleased by this arrangement, as she now had to undertake her paperwork in the small library, which was neither convenient nor comfortable. The fact that it had few books only added to her annoyance.

She was there finishing her correspondence when he barged in without a by-your-leave, and certainly without knocking.

'Amanda, come with me. I want your opinion on my plans for the Hall.'

She put down her pen, but didn't get up at his command. 'I think, Richard, that your plans are none of my concern. You are master here, and we merely your chattels.'

'That's doing it too brown, my dear. I'm certain her grace and Sarah would be happy to accompany me in your stead, if that's what you prefer.'

She stood up and came from her

position behind the table that had been fetched in especially for her to work on. 'If you put it like that, then I've no option but to come. I'll join you outside in ten minutes.'

She flew upstairs and Mary, her maid, quickly found her cloak and bonnet. She was already wearing her outdoor boots as she found indoor slippers inconvenient and cold.

He was waiting, without a coat and bareheaded, at the front door. He held out his arm and she had no option but to place her hand upon it.

'When are you planning our departure for?'

'Not for another three weeks,' she replied. 'Your fresh wardrobe will be here by then, and ours completed too. We are fortunate indeed to have our own seamstresses in-house, and an excellent milliner not far away in Ipswich town.

'I cannot tell you how happy my mother is that you have allowed her a free hand in her spending. Even Papa, who adored her, set a limit on her expenses every quarter.'

'I cannot think why that was, as there's more money in the coffers than even the most extravagant of families could spend in a lifetime. Your father was a shrewd businessman, and his investments in manufactories and shipping are proving lucrative.'

This was the first she'd heard that the Sinclair family had become involved in trade. 'Mama would be horrified to hear how our income is provided nowadays, so I suggest that we keep this to ourselves. What sort of manufactories do you own?'

'Cotton mills, ironworks, and brick kilns — there might be more, but those are the ones I've discovered so far. The family also has a considerable interest in the East India Company, as well as a fleet of their own trading vessels. I spent time in India with Sir Arthur Wellesley, and have a desire to visit the country again.'

'I told you that I don't travel, but

that's not strictly true. I've visited our estates in Scotland and the north and thoroughly enjoyed it. I also went many times with my papa to London. I should love to experience the delights of such an exotic place. Although I've read in various journals that English people suffer dreadfully from illnesses related to the heat in such places.'

'If the ladies wore sensible garments like the natives, they would get on much better. You must accompany me when I go.'

There was no time for her to respond to his outrageous suggestion, as they'd arrived at her previous home. To her surprise, there were two smartly dressed gentlemen awaiting them. They were introduced to her, but she promptly forgot their names; however, she'd gleaned that they were the architects he'd employed.

'Your grace, my lady, we've spread the plans out on the tables in the library. We're eager to hear your opinion.'

Richard nodded, and gestured that

the gentlemen lead the way, allowing them to talk in private.

'I've had them draw up plans for a new building entirely, as well as those for a complete refurbishment and modernisation of the existing one. You expressed dismay when I suggested demolishing the Hall and replacing it with something smaller and more convenient. Have you changed your mind?'

'Richard, much as I appreciate your wish to involve me in your decisions, we've no intention of living anywhere but the Dower House. Sarah might well find herself a husband soon and so could be leaving anyway. You're obliged to find yourself a suitable bride as soon as may be, and then we would have to move out anyway. Therefore, we might as well stay where we are.'

He looked at her askance. 'Are you suggesting that I'm likely to kick the bucket soon? I think that highly unlikely. If I've come through a dozen or more battles and skirmishes relatively unscathed, I hardly think I'm likely to come to grief in the peace and comfort of the English countryside.'

'Papa was in his prime when he died. You're probably not aware of this, but the Sinclair men rarely live above the age of fifty. They have a propensity to suffer from a fatal apoplexy. From what did your father die?'

He frowned. 'I've no idea, as I was already serving King and Country. But, now you come to mention it, he couldn't have been much more than fifty himself.'

Instead of being concerned or dismayed at the thought that his life could also be cut short, he grinned, making him look almost boyish.

'How old are you?'

He laughed at her directness. 'I am twenty-and-seven — my name day is in June. At your reckoning, I have another twenty or so years of healthy life ahead of me, so there's no urgency to set up my nursery as far as I can see.'

'You have exactly three-and-twenty years to establish your lineage. Surely you don't wish any son that you produce to inherit before his majority? It's imperative you marry soon and start producing sufficient sons to continue the Sinclair name.'

His eyebrows crawled beneath his hair, and she deeply regretted her intemperate words. Giving such a gentleman instruction on how he should conduct himself wasn't a sensible idea. Before he could give her the set-down she richly deserved, she attempted to snatch her arm free. His free hand gripped hers and prevented this.

'Plain speaking indeed, my dear; but as you spoke from the heart, I'll not take serious offence. However, might I suggest that you refrain from giving me orders? I don't take kindly to being told what to do by a mere slip of a girl.'

'I do apologise for speaking out of turn, your grace . . .'

His hands transferred to her elbows

and he spun her to face him. 'If you refer to me again by that ridiculous appellation, I'll not answer for the consequences. You will use my given name — is that quite clear?'

'Very well, Richard, I'll endeavour to do so. But when you look so fierce it's hard to refer to you informally. Did you know that you make me quite nervous when you're angry?'

'Then it's I who must apologise. I've spent too long giving orders and expecting them to be obeyed instantly. In future, I'll endeavour to be less dictatorial and more considerate in my dealings with you all.'

'And I promise to try and remember not to give you instructions as to what you should be doing. I know our situations are in no way similar, but for the past two years I've been in charge of the household, and also expect my wishes to be followed to the letter.'

He chuckled. 'Then that's another thing we have in common.'

She was puzzled by this remark, as

she could think of nothing else they shared.

'I was referring to our familial looks, my dear, in case you were wondering.'

* * *

Richard found this young lady a constant surprise, and the more time he spent with her the better he liked her. She was outspoken, amusing, and as sharp-witted as he was himself. He had thought her plain on first acquaintance, but that opinion had also changed. She didn't have the obvious beauty of her sisters, but she had something else, something he was finding it hard to define.

Yes — she had elegance and grace. Her looks would not fade with time, but improve. Her glorious nut-brown hair was indeed her crowning glory, and her pale green eyes were quite beautiful. God's teeth! This would not do — this would not do at all. He was her guardian, stood in the same position as her father had: he mustn't think of her

111

in any way other than as a sister.

'I think of you like my dearest sister; therefore I value your opinion above all others. I've no intention of marrying until I have to, so would be honoured and delighted to have you live with me indefinitely. Even if I do decide to raze this monstrosity to the ground, what replaces it will be more than big enough to accommodate you all, as well as any wife and children I might have in the future.'

Somehow, he'd expected her to be dismayed by his remark, but instead her smile was radiant. 'I think of you as an older brother, too. I always wanted a brother, and I know that you've had no close family to rely on.' She tilted her head, and for some reason this made his pulse leap. 'As your 'dearest sister' I'll be always on the lookout for the perfect wife for you. No, do not poker up at me, Richard. It's my job to find you someone suitable, as it is yours to keep my sisters safe from fortune-hunters and rakes.'

Amanda was glad she'd got the matter settled between them, as she was finding him a very unsettling sort of gentleman. Mind you, her experience of gentlemen of any sort was somewhat limited. For some inexplicable reason, the image of him unclothed came unbidden into her head. She released his arm as if it were red-hot, and ran up the steps in front of him and into the house as if desperate to see what changes he intended to make to her ancestral home.

In fact, she cared little about this house. Even her father, who was everything one would have expected from a Duke of Denchester, had more than once threatened to pull the house down and start again. There were so many rooms, passageways and stair-cases she was certain he had never been able to set foot in every corner of his house — she certainly hadn't.

Fortunately, by the time Richard caught up, her composure was restored and her cheeks no longer flaming.

'I'd not thought you so interested in the changes I propose, Amanda.'

'I'm not interested in changes to this inconvenient and enormous edifice, but in what you intend to replace it with.'

'Then once again, my dear, we're in complete accord. I just hope that the duchess is so easily pleased.'

The architects had overheard their conversation, and were hastily rolling up one set of plans and replacing them with another. She quite forgot her determination to keep her distance from him as they studied the exciting drawings together.

'I love this new building. Twelve apartments as well as a number of single bedchambers is more than enough. To have rooms set aside purely for bathing will be a luxury indeed.' She hurried on

114

as she realised she shouldn't have mentioned something so indelicate. 'And to have the kitchen near enough to the dining rooms for food to arrive still hot will please even my mother.'

'Come, in order to understand these more clearly we need to go outside.'

'I'm pleased that you intend to use as much of the demolished building as is possible. It will give a sense of continuity.'

They were obliged to walk through the old-fashioned parterre, and across the grass to the ornamental lake, in order to be able to see the entire house.

'The oldest part, that built in the time of Queen Elizabeth, isn't visible from the front. It's been built around, but is still there with its low ceilings and black beams. The left side was added at the time of King James, and the right more recently — about a hundred years ago, I think.'

'When was the Dower House built?'

'My grandfather replaced the original, so no more than forty years — it's positively modern compared to the rest. I cannot imagine why anyone would wish to dwell in a place the size of the Hall.'

'But surely where you are living now isn't large enough to entertain on any scale.'

'Which is a bonus as far as I'm concerned. We had a delightful gathering just before Christmas and easily accommodated forty people. I dislike anything larger than that.'

'Then you will be dreading our sojourn in London as much as I am. Does Sarah wish to find herself a husband this year, or will we have to repeat the process again next?'

'What she intends to do is to enjoy flirting and gallivanting around the place in a pretty gown — she told me that she's in no hurry to find herself a partner.'

'Tarnation take it! Are you telling me we must endure weeks of stuffy ballrooms, inane chatter and all the rest of that nonsense in order that your sister might enjoy herself?'

He sounded so disgusted that she laughed. 'Don't be so curmudgeonly, Richard. It's a rite of passage for all well-bred young ladies. Once they're married their freedom has gone — they will be more restricted than they were as daughters, and have — unless they are very lucky — an infant every year until they most likely die of exhaustion.'

For a second he thought her serious, and then he joined in her laughter. 'Are you suggesting that if I eventually enter parson's mousetrap that, when I've produced sufficient male heirs to secure the succession, I'm obliged to find myself a ladybird?'

'This is a highly unsuitable conversation for us to be having, sir. I don't know why I started it. Now, shall we return to the reason we came out here?'

They spent a further convivial time together discussing the finer points of architecture and were in complete concord about the size, positioning and shape of the future home of the Sinclairs.

'Come riding with me, Amanda; you can show me around the estate. I've spoken to my factor and perused the accounts, but I need to meet my tenants for myself.'

'Papa was a good landlord, and ensured that the well-being of his villagers and those in his employment was always taken care of.'

'That is patently obvious from what I've observed myself. Exactly how many villages are there on this estate?'

'Just the two — Denchester and Marleybridge. Denchester has around one hundred inhabitants, but Marley is more a hamlet and has less than half that number. There are a dozen farms, all profitable, and the estate stretches to over one thousand acres. Of course, I haven't included the other properties that are elsewhere in the country.'

'How can all this be run by just one person? Who has been taking care of everything in my absence?'

'Morrison is the chief factor, but he has half-a-dozen men working for him. Papa left the day-to-day running of affairs to him. The London lawyers have held the purse strings tight, not allowing me to approve any renewals or refurbishments in the neighbourhood. There will be, no doubt, many disgruntled villagers who have been awaiting repairs for too long.'

'I'd have thought there would be enough money in the coffers locally to take care of minor matters like repairing the roof of a cottage or two. This is something I'll investigate when in Town next month.'

'Now that you mention it, Richard, it's odd Morrison wasn't able to continue with his duties as he should. I wonder if he's been feathering his own nest these past two years? His father held the position for three decades, but he has only been in charge of the estate for three years, so I don't know him well.'

'I was impressed by his efficiency, but

he too will be investigated in more detail before we leave. Now, how long does it take you to change into your habit?'

'I'll be at the stables by the time both horses are tacked up and ready. Which reminds me, has your man abandoned you and returned to his military life?'

'Not at all. He's gone to London on business for me. In future he will be my man of affairs. I've appointed the young man you sent to me as my permanent valet.'

'James will be thrilled at his elevation. He's worked for the family since he was a boot boy, and his father before him.'

He checked his pocket watch — not gold, but silver, and looking sadly the worse for wear. She would give him Papa's gold watch — he was the duke now, and must look the part.

★  ★  ★

There was no need for Richard to make his way around to the stables for half an hour at least, as he knew full well that he was in for a considerable wait. Ladies took an unconscionable time to change their raiment, and he was certain Amanda was no different.

He went in search of the architects in order to ensure that they knew exactly what they were to do. After a lengthy discussion about the merits of various local builders and labourers, he spoke to the housekeeper and butler. They seemed somewhat startled when he informed them that the house must be emptied of furniture from top to bottom.

'Yes, your grace, but where would you like us to put everything whilst the new house is built?'

'By the time it's all wrapped in cloth of some sort and brought down to the entrance hall, I shall have found a place where it can be stored for the next year or so.' The housekeeper looked unconvinced, but curtsied and hurried away to get things set in motion.

The butler remained behind. He

looked uncomfortable. 'What is it, man? Don't dither about — tell me at once what's bothering you.'

'I should like to tender my resignation, your grace. I don't want to be here when this magnificent building is knocked down.'

'I understand why you wish to go. I'll see you have a decent pension, and somewhere warm and comfortable to live out your days.'

The old man bowed. 'I thank you, your grace; your generosity is much appreciated. I shall remain to oversee the packing, but will depart as soon as that is completed, if that is acceptable to you?'

Although some of the reception rooms were sparsely furnished, they were still going to need an enormous barn of some sort to store everything. He'd yet to explore the attics, and there was usually a plethora of interesting items hiding up there.

He was about to go to investigate the uppermost regions of this vast place when he heard the distinct clatter of horses approaching. He wasn't expecting visitors, so who the hell could it be?

He wandered to the front door and to his astonishment saw Amanda, riding astride her stallion and leading the chestnut gelding he'd brought back from the stud the other day. He wasn't sure which bothered him the most — the fact that she'd appeared so swiftly, or that she was riding like a gentleman and not using a side-saddle.

She tossed him his reins. He gathered them up and sprung into the saddle without comment.

'If you're looking so poker-faced because I'm riding like this, then firstly, it's none of your business; and secondly, this is a divided skirt made especially for me, and not an iota of ankle will be visible.'

He reached out and grabbed Othello's bit, bringing the stallion hard up against his own mount. 'I don't give a damn what saddle you use here, but anywhere else you'll ride as expected.'

He had her full attention and chose his words carefully. 'Until you reach your majority, I am your legal guardian and you're my responsibility. You will do as I say. I suggest that you bear that in mind.'

He released her horse, and it took off from a standstill to an extended canter in one smooth movement, leaving him to stare in admiration at her horsemanship.

He urged Rufus, his gelding, after her, and they thundered across the grass at a flat gallop. Despite his expertise he wasn't gaining an inch. She vanished down a narrow path between the trees. She had run mad — to travel at breakneck speed between trees might well prove fatal for both rider and horse.

He slowed his pace a little and entered the woodland, expecting to see her on the dirt ahead of him. Instead, what he saw was an empty track and no sign of her at all. He reined back to a sensible pace and examined the soft ground for evidence of hoofprints. These were easy to track and he followed them, not sure if his tension was caused by fury or anxiety.

After half a mile the track widened and divided, one part going right, the other left. He was leaning from the saddle, searching for clues as to which path she'd taken, when Rufus shied and he pitched headfirst to the ground. Instinctively, he curled and landed on his shoulders — his dignity the only part of him that was hurt.

He rolled to his feet and brushed the dirt from his person. He'd committed the cardinal sin of releasing his hold on the reins. Rufus was nowhere in sight. He cursed under his breath as he examined the churned-up ground in an attempt to distinguish the hoofprints of his horse from that of hers.

This was an impossible task. He was standing in the centre of the track when she appeared on the right-hand path, leading his errant gelding.

'Are you hurt? What happened? Was

it my fault you took a fall?'

She dropped from the saddle and handed him his reins. Her anxiety was genuine, and this touched him deeply.

'It was my own stupidity, sweetheart. I was leaning down when a pheasant flew up beneath our feet, and you can imagine what happened next.'

'Then it was my fault, and you have every right to be angry with me. I'm not known for my impetuosity, sir, and have no notion why I behaved as I did. I do know better than to travel through trees at speed, and I'm lucky not to have broken my neck by doing so.'

'I'm not angry anymore. Shall we remount, and then you can direct us to the village?' He turned his back on her, not offering to take her boot and toss her into the saddle as he wanted to see if she would ask for his help.

When he glanced over his shoulder, she was already mounted and smiling sweetly at him.

'If we take the left-hand path, it leads to the village. There's a stile we have to jump into a field, but I'm sure that will prove no obstacle to either of us.'

★ ★ ★

Amanda was beginning to understand him better now and in future would do her best to avoid doing anything that might make him angry. He couldn't be considered a close relation, but he was head of the family, and if he wished to, he could make all their lives unpleasant.

Perhaps she should have asked him to help her into the saddle and not been so independent — too late to repine — she would do her best to smooth things over between them during their ride.

'The female guerrillas — and there are many — in Spain wear a similar garment to yours. They all ride astride, as it's safer when going up the steep mountain tracks.'

'I saw an illustration of one such garment in a journal of my father's, and had my seamstress copy it. My horse

127

goes as well under a side-saddle as he does with this.'

'I've been thinking about our transfer next month — would you like to take your stallion?'

'I should love to, but I think it better not. What's acceptable on one's own demesne will be frowned upon in Town.'

'Then what will you ride when you go out with me?'

She was surprised that he intended to spend so much time with her, and wasn't sure if this was sensible or not. 'Last time I was there, my father hired hacks for us. Sarah doesn't care to ride, but she does enjoy going out in an open carriage, as does Beth.'

'We can hardly travel all the way in one — is it possible to hire what you want?'

'There's a high-perch phaeton, a brougham and a curricle in the coach house there. Papa was an excellent whipster and often took me out in the phaeton.' She hesitated before she revealed that she too could handle the reins as well as anyone. However, this observant gentleman immediately recognised her reluctance to continue, and correctly interpreted the reason.

'Do you drive?'

'I do, and have even handled a four-in-hand, but I prefer to drive a smaller vehicle rather than a travelling carriage. In case you're wondering, I only drove in London at dawn when nobody was around to see.'

'Then I suggest that we continue this practice. However, I've no intention of allowing you to handle the reins of the phaeton, whatever your father might have done.'

She raised her whip and pointed to the hedge with the stile which could now be seen in the distance. 'Fortunately, one can see if pedestrians are approaching from the village before one jumps.' She stood in her stirrups and demonstrated her words. 'The field is clear — it's safe to go.'

It didn't occur to her that he might

prefer to take the lead, so she settled down into the saddle, squeezed, and her horse moved smoothly forward. Othello had taken this jump dozens of times and there was no need for her to interfere. He knew exactly what to do. His stride lengthened and she gave him his head. They soared over the stile and landed neatly on the other side.

Richard followed suit, and side by side they cantered towards the distant village.

'I know nothing about my properties apart from what I've picked up from the accounts. Tell me what I'll see here.'

'There's a blacksmith, a baker, a cobbler and a general store. We have labourers and carpenters living here as well. In fact, there's little we need to send out for.'

'Who supplies them with fresh milk, vegetables, meat, etcetera?'

'They can purchase what they need from our home farm — which is where everything for our family is produced. I take it that you have seen our magnificent kitchen garden? All the vegetables for the staff and family are grown in abundance there.'

'I admired it, as well as the carp pool, trout stream, and the yard full of fat hens and cockerels. I take it there are deer and game birds in the woods that surround the Hall?'

'Yes, we've always been self-sufficient where food's concerned, and the surplus is distributed to all those on the estate. Although they have sufficient land to grow their own, keep a pig, and enough chickens to provide them with meat and eggs.'

\* \* \*

The visit to the village went well, as Richard was used to dealing with his subordinates from his time in the army. His manner was perfect, friendly but not informal — exactly what was expected of him. Despite their concern that the estate manager had not been doing his duty there were few complaints.

'Do you wish to return the same way, or shall I take you by a different route?'

'The most direct — there are things I need to do before we dine this evening. Which reminds me: in future, I don't wish to keep country hours and eat so early. It makes sense to adjust, as once we're in Town things will have to change.'

'I'm surprised that you know such things, as you've been at pains to tell us all that you spent your entire life as a soldier and have no knowledge of how things are done in the *ton*.'

'As an officer, I was expected to mingle with the aristocracy and grand folk that congregate around a successful campaign. If you're concerned that I'll cause you embarrassment by my behaviour, you can rest easy.' He swivelled in the saddle, and his smile made her toes curl. 'That said, I've no intention of behaving like one of those so-called gentlemen who've never done

anything useful in their lives. I don't
gamble, don't drink to excess, and have
no intention of seducing any young
ladies or setting up a mistress in a
convenient house nearby.'

# 8

Richard was still amused by Amanda's
shocked expression as he strolled into
the house. He walked to the study
from which he had ousted her, but
felt not a pang of guilt. There was a
pile of correspondence waiting to be
dealt with, and with a sigh of
resignation he sat down at the desk and
began to read.

He supposed that a true gentleman
would have gone immediately to his
rooms and removed the stink of the
stable from his person. He'd stuck his
hands under the stable pump, and that
would have to do. This constant urge
to change one's clothes at every
opportunity was something he refused
to adopt. No doubt the ladies had so
little to do with their time, they were
happy to have the opportunity to
change their ensemble several times a

day. Good God — they even made morning calls after lunch — that was a nonsense if ever he'd heard one!

He was immersed in his work when there was a sharp knock on the door, and he barked a command to enter.

'I apologise for intruding, your grace, but I've just got back from Horse Guards and need to speak to you most urgently.' Riley was standing in the doorway, swaying with fatigue and decidedly travel-stained.

'Come in, my friend, take a seat and I'll send for refreshments.'

'I ain't fit to sit in here, your grace . . .'

'It's up to me who sits where and in what condition. Find yourself somewhere comfortable before you collapse at my feet.'

He yanked the bell-strap and waited at the door to give his orders. 'Tell me what's so urgent you've arrived almost on your knees.'

'It's like this, sir — they've no choice but to accept your resignation, but they

135

ain't going to take mine. I've got three months, two weeks and four days left to serve, and they intend I'll return to Spain or be declared a deserter.'

'You'll do no such thing.' He'd left the door open, and the rattle of crockery on a tray alerted him that they were no longer able to speak freely. He gestured to the footman to put the food and coffee on the desk and then waved him out.

'Help yourself, Riley, I'll share the coffee, but as we dine at a ridiculously early hour, I won't have the sandwiches and cake.'

He poured himself a coffee and wandered to the far end of the room to drink it whilst Riley devoured the food. There was a soft tap on the door and he guessed who it was.

He opened it himself. 'Excellent! Amanda, I have a conundrum, and hope you can solve it for me.'

She waved to Riley that he didn't need to get up, but continue his meal, and then joined Richard by the window.

'I'm sorry I interrupted you — but how can I help?'

'First, what can I help *you* with? I hope there's nothing untoward going on that I must deal with.'

'No. I just came to tell you that I've spoken with Cook, and dinner will be served fashionably late in future. Mama thought it a sensible notion, much to my surprise, and agreed with alacrity, on the condition that we change. Not into full evening dress, so don't look so horrified. Just something a little smarter than day clothes.'

'That seems acceptable. I'll be sharp-set by then, as I failed to eat luncheon at midday.'

'I'm sure a man who's used to bivouacking in the desert with only a spoonful of water and a crust of bread to keep him going will manage perfectly well until this evening. Now, how can I be of assistance?'

He smiled at her wit but refused to be drawn into riposting. He explained the dilemma, and she turned and stared at Riley with her lips pursed.

'Your man is intelligent, I'm certain he could adopt the speech of a gentleman if so wished. All he needs is a wardrobe to match his elevated status, and I doubt that even his friends will recognise him.'

'His real name is O'Riley — he's Irish, but thought it better not to draw attention to the fact whilst he was serving in the King's army. He dropped his accent, and no one has ever suspected the truth.'

Her delighted smile made him feel like a giant among men.

'Mr O'Riley, from this moment forward you will be a gentleman of modest means who is employed by his grace as his man of business. From what I've just been told, you will have no difficulty adapting your manners and mode of speech.'

He was already on his feet, and bowed. 'My lady, Patrick O'Riley at your service. I cannot tell you how delighted I am to be here.'

Amanda clapped her hands like a child. 'That's capital! If anyone comes looking then we can tell them no one called Riley is residing here, and that will be no more than the truth.'

'By God, O'Riley, you're a better mimic than I realised. You were gone an unconscionable time, so I assume your smart wardrobe will be arriving here soon?'

'Not only mine, your grace, but your own. The trunks travelled by the common stage and a local carter will bring them. I reckon I'll be smart as paint by tomorrow at the latest.'

He'd had no difficulty maintaining his genteel diction, which was impressive. 'As you were here no more than one night, I doubt that the staff will recall how you spoke or what your name was.'

O'Riley's grin was broad as he bowed to both of them. 'Thank you, my lady, your grace. I'll not let either of you down.' He took himself off to clean up, leaving Richard alone with Amanda.

'Will he now be part of the family and dine with us, or does he remain below stairs? I've no idea of the etiquette in such a matter.'

'He's in an invidious position, neither fish nor fowl. Mama's companion, and the governess we had, were also marooned somewhere between the servants' hall and the family. He will dine with the housekeeper and butler, or in his room with a tray on most nights. However, he can be included in social events and to make up the numbers at dinner.'

'I think it's safer, at least until after his enlistment has expired, that he remains out of public view. Even clean-shaven, with hair cut short and a gentleman's appearance, anybody who served with him would immediately know who he was. The man's more than two yards high in his stockinged feet, and having blazing red hair will mark him out at once.'

'That's easily remedied, Richard. I'll go at once and find the walnut juice that my papa used to cover the grey in his hair. We can do nothing about his size, but with brown hair I think we'll get by.'

* ★ ★

Amanda found the required item and sent Mary, her abigail, to deliver it. Then she went in search of her sister, for if this masquerade was to be successful, both Sarah and Mama must go along with it. Beth was rarely in company, and she doubted she would have remembered Mr O'Riley's name anyway.

She discovered them in the small drawing room. This was on the south side of the house and less formal than the larger one they had been using. They were looking through the pile of acceptances that had been arriving for the ball that was to be held in the first week of May.

'There you are, my dear, you will be pleased that so far there have been no refusals. Also, on this other pile are the stack of invitations for us to attend similar events. I suppose we must obtain Richard's consent before we accept any.'

'I doubt that he'll care about such things, but it would be wise not to make assumptions in this matter. I've discovered he can be quite alarming when his opinions are disregarded.'

Her sister gave her a most particular look. 'I cannot think how or why you might have experienced this. I thought the two of you were the best of friends.'

'We are, Sarah, but I have an unfortunate tendency to speak to him as if he was under my command rather than the other way around. Shall we talk of something else? I must tell you that this family is now involved in the most exciting venture.'

Her mother put down the letter she was perusing. 'Go on, do not keep us in suspense, my dear.'

They thought that harbouring Mr O'Riley was an excellent decision.

'I intend to do my best to trip him up and make him revert to his Irish or common diction. It will be most entertaining to do so.'

'I doubt that you'll have much opportunity, sister, as Richard has instructed him to keep out of sight as much as possible.'

'He can do so here, but what about when we're in Town?'

'By then he will have mastered his new persona, and there'll be no danger of anyone thinking he's anyone but the Duke of Denchester's confidante and man of affairs.'

The next hour passed pleasantly enough, and when it was time to change for dinner she had made a list of all those who wished to attend Sarah's debut ball, and another of those who'd invited them to a variety of social events. Her mother had arranged these in order of precedence, with those from the most prestigious families at the top.

As Amanda shared an apartment with her sister they walked upstairs together. They had separate bedchambers but a sitting room in common.

'If I'm to attend even half those invitations, I'll scarcely have time to sleep!' Sarah reflected. 'I'm now beginning to regret I insisted on this Season.'

'You don't have to go to everything, my love, only those that appeal to you. I'm certain there will be time for visiting the sights, driving out and making morning calls on those we wish to further our acquaintance with.'

'What if I meet a gentleman who wants to marry me?'

'I should think you'll meet several. After all, isn't that the object of the exercise? You're a beautiful, titled heiress. Remember, they have to have Richard's approval before they can address you. I'm certain that if you don't wish to become betrothed to anyone this year, he will support you.'

'It should be your debut, not mine. After all, you're almost two years my senior.'

'You know my opinion on this

matter. I've been out for three years, so can attend any function and wear colours. It's fortunate that pastel shades are perfect on you.'

'But you do intend to come with me and Mama to everything, don't you? We both know that our mother will spend the entire evening playing cards and take no notice whatsoever of our behaviour.'

'I'll sit with the other chaperones. I can assure you that Richard will be keeping a very close eye on you and those that you dance with. No fortune-hunter, rake or other undesirable will be allowed within arm's distance of you.'

'But what if someone asks you to dance?'

'Richard and I have agreed that we shall dance once with each other and then he will dance once with you — after that, we intend to remain at the edge of the ballroom, keeping a close eye on you and your partners.'

For some reason this information

delighted her sister. 'I'll say no more about it, then. Have you decided what you're going to wear tonight?'

'Mary will have set something out for me. I'll be ready far quicker than you, so I'll go down first if you have no objection?'

'You go ahead, Amanda. I'll wait for our mama.'

'I'll go and see Beth before I go down — she rarely gets the opportunity to see us in anything but plain gowns.'

Her sister was already in bed looking through a picture book. 'That's a pretty gown, Amanda, that funny green colour exactly matches your eyes.'

'Thank you, darling. I thought to take you out in the carriage tomorrow — would you like that?'

'I would, I would! Can I wear a new gown too?'

'You must wear something suitable for travelling in an open carriage, Beth. I'm sure that Nanny will find you something perfect.'

She kissed her sister and left her

happily planning her ensemble for the next day.

There was no one in the drawing room — but then she hadn't expected there to be as she was half an hour ahead of the appointed time. She decided to use the interim to play a new piece that had arrived from London a few days ago.

As always, she was immediately lost in the music. Her fingers flew across the keyboard and she scarcely needed to look at the sheet in front of her. She was fortunate indeed that she could play a piece through once or twice and then have it down perfectly.

At the end, she sat for a few seconds as the notes faded away. Richard spoke from behind her, making her almost fall off the piano stool.

'That was quite superb, I've never heard anyone play so well. I've not heard it before — is it a new concerto?'

She closed the piano with a decided snap and slid out from behind the stool. 'For a large gentleman you are remarkably soft-footed. That might be an advantage for a soldier but is a disagreeable trait for a gentleman.' She spoke with her back to him — somehow it was easier to be cross when she couldn't see him.

'My dear girl, if you wish to take me to task then I'd much prefer it if I could see your face. By the by, that's a remarkably pretty gown: the colour matches your eyes exactly.'

She spun so quickly she almost lost her balance. His lightning reactions prevented her from a nasty tumble.

'Were you eavesdropping on my conversation with my sister, sir? That's exactly what she said.'

He looked somewhat startled by her vehemence but rallied wonderfully. 'Then Sarah and I are in complete agreement. And, no, I certainly didn't stand listening outside your door.'

'Then how did you know that my gown matches my eyes before I turned to face you?'

'Is that what's put a bee under your

bonnet? Our colouring is identical. Pale green is my eye colour too. Are you not going to return the compliment?'

A strange bubbling excitement filled her chest. She felt like a small child when she spoke to him in this light-hearted way. She increased the distance between them so she could look at him in full.

He was wearing an immaculate green topcoat, square-cut in the modern fashion, with two rows of smart brass buttons and a rolled collar. His white shirt and snowy neckcloth drew attention to the strong column of his neck. She daren't move her eyes one iota lower as it would remind her of what she'd seen that she should not have done.

\* \* \*

Richard rather enjoyed her scrutiny, and was amused by the fact her gaze travelled no lower than his shirt. Seeing him naked had obviously had more effect than he'd thought at the time. The kind of women he was used to saw men unclothed every day of the week — there was no privacy in an army camp. Sometimes, when he was lucky, he'd been billeted in a decent house in a village, but not when they were on the move.

'I can hear the others coming. Allow me to escort you to the other end of the drawing room.' He held out his arm. For a second, she hesitated; then, with some reluctance, placed her hand on it.

'I think you are under a serious misapprehension if you believe that I need to be treated like a shy young debutante. I'm perfectly capable of walking from one end of the room to the other without your assistance.'

'I'm well aware of that, my dear. I doubt that a young lady of the sort you describe would ride the way you do. Or, for that matter, play with such passion and virtuosity.'

This compliment obviously pleased

her as her cheeks glowed and her eyes were sparkling when she looked up at him.

'I've had the best tuition over the years as my father loved to hear me play. He would accompany me on the fiddle, and my sisters and my mama would sing.'

He was used to seeing the duchess in full evening rig, as she'd insisted on changing every night despite the fact that no one else did. Tonight, she had dressed down. Her silk gown was a startling shade of puce but, apart from that, was perfectly acceptable. Sarah was wearing a simple, but fetching, muslin in a pretty forget-me-not blue.

'I am surrounded by a bevy of beautiful ladies tonight. I could almost get to enjoy this changing for dinner nonsense.'

'I'm absolutely ravenous, Richard, I would have eaten more at luncheon if I'd known I was to wait so long for my dinner,' Sarah said with a smile.

'To mention such a thing, my dear, is

not considered polite in mixed company. A young lady must never be hungry or thirsty — or at least must never say so.'

'I wouldn't dream of doing so, Mama, anywhere else but with my family.'

Amanda nodded towards the door where the butler was hovering, waiting to announce that dinner was served. Tonight the meal was more elaborate, three courses each with three removes — but nothing smothered in the rich cream sauces which Richard so disliked.

As always, the entire party moved into the drawing room when the meal was done. 'Will you play that new piece, Amanda? Or something else if you don't wish to perform that one again,' he said.

This time, when she finished, he led them in a round of applause, and even her mother was enthusiastic. 'I think we should hold a musical evening so that you can demonstrate your ability on the pianoforte, my dear.'

'As that is a more informal occasion, Mama, we can decide when we arrive. I should like to go to Vauxhall Gardens and see the firework display, and I'm sure Beth would enjoy it. It's something she can participate in without being overwhelmed.'

'As long as dear Richard is prepared to accompany us then I can see no objection to that particular excursion. There are certain parts of the garden where no respectable young lady would promenade, but as long as we stay together with our footmen and escort all should be well.'

He was handed the list of invitations and looked through them in bewilderment. 'I've heard of none of these people — I haven't moved in such elevated circles before. I must trust to your good judgement, your grace, and allow you to make the decision as to where we go.'

'Thank you, Richard, I had hoped you would take that line. I think that attending three evening events in one week will be more than sufficient. That will leave time for morning calls, visits to the circulating library and drives in the park.'

'That sounds wonderful. Our new ensembles should begin to arrive tomorrow. We'll be in the first stare of fashion when we go — not that we aren't very fine already.'

'Sarah, I do hope you do not intend to puff yourself up in that way when we are at a social event. If you wish to take a husband, then you must be modest and polite at all times.'

'I'll not let you down, Mama, I give you my word. I do know how to go on, as Miss Westley was an excellent teacher.'

'I thought that Miss Westley might be asked to act as your companion until your own returns, Mama,' Amanda immediately suggested.

'I should like that above all things: she was a very respectful and pleasant young lady when she was here last time.

She might have made a satisfactory marriage if her parents had not perished from the influenza.'

'Then, please excuse me, I'll write to her at once. We have remained in regular correspondence, and I know the family she's been with these past two years are moving to Scotland, but she has no wish to go with them.'

# 9

The next few weeks flew past, and Amanda was now eager to depart. The demolition of the big house was underway: the air was full of dust, and nowhere could anyone find a moment's peace and quiet during daylight hours.

The servants had departed several days ago, their luggage yesterday, and today they would finally be on their way. She was up betimes and went in search of her cousin.

'I do wish I could ride alongside you, Richard, I hate being bounced around in a closed carriage for hours on end.'

'Then do so. As long as you're prepared to ride side-saddle, then I've no objection, and would enjoy the company. Actually, it makes more sense for you to ride your stallion rather than a groom.'

'Thank you. I left out my habit in the

hope that you would agree to my suggestion. I'll be ready long before the carriages leave.'

On her way to change — without the assistance of her maid — she met Sarah and Beth. 'Where are you going, Amanda? The carriage is waiting and Papa always said horses should not be allowed to stand about at our convenience.'

'That's very true, sweetheart, but Richard has given me permission to ride with him and I'm going immediately to change into my habit.'

Her sister pouted and for a horrible moment Amanda thought there might be a dreadful scene. Sarah stepped in quickly to distract Beth.

'There will be so much more room with just the two of us in the carriage. You can stretch out in comfort on one side, and I can do so on the other.'

Beth swung her favourite doll around in excitement. 'I like that. Why doesn't our mama want to be in the same carriage as us?'

'She's an indifferent traveller, and only needs the comfort and support of Miss Westley on the long journey.'

When she reappeared the carriages were just pulling away, and one of the remaining grooms was holding the reins of her horse. Richard was also unmounted.

'Allow me to assist you into the saddle, cousin.'

She turned her back, bent her leg and he tossed her up. When she'd finished settling herself safely, she looked up to find him already mounted and watching her with a slight smile.

'I thought we could go across country — O'Riley has given me directions so we can meet with the carriages in Colchester.'

'As long as we remain there to allow the horses to rest, I can see no objection to that. I helped to school your gelding and I warn you that he has the most enormous jump.'

His teeth flashed white in his tanned face. 'I discovered that to my cost the

158

other day. I almost went head-first into the ditch.'

'I'm surprised O'Riley didn't wish to join us on horseback. He doesn't seem the sort of gentleman to enjoy being inside a carriage.'

'He's escorting several boxes of important papers that I cannot allow to remain unsupervised. It will be a new experience for him, and good practice in his new persona as a gentleman.'

There were two grooms accompanying them, but they remained a respectful distance behind.

★　★　★

He'd never spent so long in the company of any female, and the more he did the better he liked her. Naturally, he'd talked with ladies before, but until now had never had a proper conversation.

The carriages wouldn't arrive at the Red Lion in Colchester for another hour at least. This was beneficial as it meant their horses would have ample time to recuperate before they completed the second half of today's journey. The teams pulling the carriages travelled at a slower pace, but they would also need rest before continuing.

'There are chambers reserved for us at the Saracens Inn in Chelmsford for tonight. It's around thirty miles, so we should complete it easily in three hours, although the carriages will take longer.'

'I've never spent so long in the saddle, but so far am suffering no ill effects. I didn't like to hunt. However, that would have been an opportunity to spend several hours galloping around the countryside.'

'If at any time you wish to join your sisters in the carriage, you can do so. One of the grooms can lead your horse.'

'They'd be better riding him and leading their own, as Othello doesn't like to be led.' She was on the ground before he could offer to assist her. 'But I've no intention of being so feeble

— once I make up my mind to do a thing, I always complete it. Therefore, I'll remain by your side.'

He was inordinately pleased by this declaration and he'd no notion why this should be so. He was perfectly content with his own company as a rule.

At the Red Lion, there were two chambers put aside for their use — one for the ladies and one for himself.

'Do we eat upstairs or is there a private parlour down here?'

'The snug has been reserved for us. There'll be a cold collation waiting when we're ready.'

'I should dearly like to visit the castle as I've heard talk of it being of Norman origin. Quite unique and of the same age as the White Tower in London. Do you think it will raise a few eyebrows if we go in our riding clothes?'

He chuckled. 'It would raise far more if we went in without them.' He regretted his remark when he saw her distress. Before she could rush off, he took her elbow and guided her from under the archway and out into the street.

'Amanda, that was insensitive and boorish. I've never apologised for what happened just after I arrived. I didn't think to see me as you did would cause you so much embarrassment and upset. I sincerely apologise. I give you my word nothing of the sort will ever happen again.' Her head remained lowered. 'Please, sweetheart, look at me.'

When she remained looking firmly at the ground, he reached out and with his gloved finger gently raised her chin. Something odd happened when he saw her tear-filled eyes. In that moment all he wanted was to stand as her protector, keep her safe from harm, and never cause her to cry again because of him.

'Thank you for your apology, Richard. I wish I didn't find such things so upsetting. I expect unclothed people are a common thing in the hurly-burly of an army camp. But even a married lady would never see their husband as I saw you that day.'

He stared at her, and was about to explain exactly what took place between a man and a woman in the marriage bed, but bit back the words. Small wonder she was unable to get the image of him naked out of her head when she had such an erroneous idea of the married state.

She tilted her head in order to look at him more closely. 'From your expression, I've said something you vehemently disagree with. Now I'm intrigued, and I insist that you explain what it is you're keeping from me.'

It was his turn to flush — not something he recalled doing since he was a child. He ran his finger around his neckcloth, which had become inexplicably too tight. 'The castle is a short distance to the right. You can see it above the houses.'

She didn't press him to answer, and without him having to suggest it slipped her hand through his arm. 'Then we shall go and look together and ignore any of the local populace who think it odd of us to be walking when we're wearing our riding clothes.'

They viewed the castle and were both impressed. 'I'm disappointed that we can't go inside today — I gather that there are conducted tours sometimes that allow one to do so.'

'Colchester appears to be a prosperous town. There seems to be an abundance of soldiers in their smart red coats — is there a barracks nearby?'

'This town relies heavily on the army for its wealth. Don't ask me to escort you there as I shall refuse.'

Her laugh turned several heads. It was the first time he'd heard her laugh out loud, and it was a lovely sound. 'Come, I'm hungry,' he said. 'I expect the carriages have arrived and your mother will be wondering where we are.'

They were just approaching the entrance to the inn when someone hailed him from across the road. 'Good

Lord — I never thought to see you here, Sinclair. Have you been sent to collect more men for your brigade?'

Lord Percy Hetherington, a fellow officer in his old regiment, strode towards him, hand outheld. Dammit to hell! The last thing he wanted was to introduce Amanda or reveal that he was now the Duke of Denchester. He considered himself quick-witted but could come up with nothing to avoid the inevitable.

He shook Percy's hand and then had no option but to introduce his companion. 'Lord Hetherington, allow me to introduce you to Lady Amanda Sinclair.'

She curtsied, but not deeply, and he bowed. He was about to whisk her away when she spoke. 'Lord Hetherington, I am delighted to make your acquaintance. You are the first person from his military life that my cousin, his grace the Duke of Denchester, has been able to introduce me to.'

'So that's why you vanished from

Town. Congratulations, old fellow, you'll make an excellent fist of your new post. Excuse me, my lady, your grace, I am already running late for an important rendezvous.'

He watched his erstwhile friend stride away and cursed the ill fortune that had brought them face-to-face. Fond as he was of Percy, the man was an inveterate gossip. By this evening word would have spread that he was walking unchaperoned with Amanda. God knows what the duchess would say when she heard of it — and the gossip was bound to reach London eventually.

Too bad — he would deal with the repercussions when they happened. The most important thing was to get her safely inside before anyone else he knew accosted them and wished to be introduced.

\* \* \*

Amanda was at a loss to know why he almost bundled her back under the archway and into the building. What was the urgency? There was no sign of the family carriages, so they weren't tardy.

He snapped his fingers and a maid ran over and curtsied. 'Take us to the chambers that have been set aside for our use.'

'Yes, your grace, if you would care to please follow me.'

The room allocated for her use overlooked the main street. She dismissed the girl who was eager to assist in her ablutions. She was quite capable of washing her own face and hands, and sponging off the worst of the dirt from her skirts.

She was admiring the view from the window when someone knocked on the door. She hurried across to open it and found him standing there.

'Richard, are we to go down? I thought we would wait until the others were here before we had luncheon.'

He ignored her remark and entered without asking for permission. His face was grave. Something had either upset or angered him and he'd obviously come to tell her what it was.

'I shouldn't have been walking with you without a chaperone. Hetherington will be spreading the word throughout Colchester, and you can be certain rumours will reach London soon enough.'

'I don't know why you're so cross about it, Richard. It's perfectly permissible for a guardian to escort his ward to view the sights. Good heavens — even my mama will have no objection when she hears.'

He began to look a little less grim. 'But Hetherington doesn't know the facts and will embellish them to suit himself.'

'Then I suggest, if you're concerned, that you go after him and put him straight.'

She finally grasped why he'd been so agitated — he'd come to the ludicrous conclusion that she was compromised and he would have to offer to marry

168

her. Small wonder he was upset at such a thing. He would never wish to marry a plain beanpole of a girl such as herself when he could have any unattached young lady that he wanted. He must be the most eligible parti in the country. She was certain that it wasn't often that a duke became available on the marriage mart, and for one to be as young and personable as he was made him even more desirable to the matchmaking mothers.

He shrugged. 'Are you worried about it?'

'Good heavens, not at all. Our behaviour was above reproach. We might not have had a chaperone but we were in full view, of anyone who cared to look, at all times.' She was about to reassure him that he had no need to worry he was going to have to make her an offer, then decided that would be presumptuous.

'Then, Amanda, I'll see you downstairs. I expect the duchess and your sisters will be here at any moment.'

'Wait, I'll come with you. I much prefer to be in the fresh air than cooped up in here.'

They had just stepped through the door when the rattle of a carriage entering at the far end of the archway made them both look round.

'Excellent, the carriages have come at last. If you show the ladies where they can refresh themselves, the sooner we'll get our meal and be able to set out for Chelmsford.'

'I take it that Mr O'Riley will not be joining us?'

'His carriage will stop at the next town where there's no danger of anyone recognising him.'

He left her to greet her family and he wandered inside to alert the landlord that they would require their luncheon in a quarter of an hour. The grooms would take care of the horses and they had sufficient coinage to purchase themselves something substantial to eat.

Being a duke wasn't a lot different

from being an officer — his duty was to take care of those who depended on him as well as make sure everything necessary was done on time.

\* \* \*

The duchess was surprisingly buoyant considering he'd been told she was a poor traveller. She certainly ate with gusto as did everybody else. He thought the appointment, even if it was temporary, of Miss Westley an ideal arrangement. The young woman was articulate, pleasant and obviously a great favourite with the family.

'I shall leave you ladies to get yourself organised for our departure. I'm going to instruct the grooms to harness the teams and saddle our horses.'

'How long do we have before we must leave?' Sarah asked.

'Half an hour — that's more than enough time.'

The duchess was prune-faced and obviously intended to protest, so he took himself off before she could argue.

He overheard Amanda speaking to her mother. 'Richard expects his instructions to be followed to the letter, Mama, so I suggest that you don't keep him waiting or you might find yourself abandoned here.'

He was smiling when he walked out. In fact, he had found himself doing that a lot lately. He wasn't known for being a man of good humour. He was an excellent leader, a good tactician, and led his men from the front. But there was rarely much to smile about on a battlefield.

★ ★ ★

As before, he and Amanda arrived ahead of the others at their overnight destination in Chelmsford.

'This Saracens seems a superior sort of place,' she commented. 'I'm surprised to find something so luxurious in a town as small as this.'

'It's fortuitous, my dear, I merely

sent the groom last week to make the reservation. It could have been a hovel for all I knew.'

She smiled at him. 'I hardly think a duke's servant would reserve anywhere but the very best for his master.'

This time he dismounted with alacrity and was at her side before she could kick her foot free of the single stirrup iron. 'Allow me to assist you down, Amanda. You must be weary after so many hours in the saddle.'

She didn't protest, and he reached up and placed his hands around her waist. He was shocked at how slender this was. He lifted her and she weighed no more than a sack of coal. He couldn't help laughing at his comparison.

'Kindly share the joke, sir, I don't wish to be left out of any merriment.'

*  *  *

She thought he wasn't going to tell her but then he changed his mind. 'I was thinking that for a tall young woman

173

you weigh nothing at all — in my mind I compared you to a sack of coal. And then thought how inappropriate that comparison was.'

'I suppose you could have thought of something less industrial. However, I'm flattered that you think me light. I can only think this is because you're such a large person yourself that it makes me seem insignificant beside you.'

'You are never that, sweetheart. You and your family have become dear to me in these past weeks. I've made myself a vow that I'll never let anything or anyone harm you.'

His sincerity touched a chord within her. 'Then I thank you, Richard. You might be only distantly related to us, but as far as we're concerned, you're now a much-loved and respected head of the family.'

Their tête-à-tête was interrupted by the arrival of two obsequious ostlers. He tossed them the reins of both horses, held out his arm imperiously, and she placed her gloved hand upon it.

Together they sailed in as if they were far more important than they actually were.

'I suppose we're the nearest they've ever had to a member of the royal family. I expect they'd be disappointed if we were less than haughty in our dealings with them.' She spoke quietly so no one could overhear her. His arm trembled beneath her fingers and she knew he was trying hard not to laugh.

They were met by a tall, thin gentleman — if he could be called such when he was the landlord — immaculate in black so that he resembled a butler. He too bowed as if to a king and queen.

'Welcome, your grace, my lady, I cannot tell you how honoured we are to have you stay with us. Our best chambers have been set aside for your use. I shall take you up myself if you would care to follow me.'

# 10

Amanda had never ridden through the streets of London, so this was an interesting experience for her. The fact that she knew the city far better than her companion was another thing that delighted her.

It was fortunate indeed that neither of their mounts were skittish as the constant racket of passing diligences, hackney cabs, and men and women shouting their wares might have upset less well-schooled horses.

'Things will improve from now on, Richard, I expect you're relieved to get away from the smell and noise of the East End.'

'I prefer to be amongst ordinary folk and, to be honest, I'm dreading spending the next few weeks when I'll have to rub shoulders with the toplofty. Apart from Perry, I've not met another

176

aristocrat that I didn't want to flatten for his stupidity.'

'In which case, sir, I'll insist that you keep your hands firmly behind your back at all times so nothing untoward takes place.'

'An excellent suggestion, my dear, apart from the fact that doing so would preclude me from dancing with you or your sister.'

The more time she spent in his company the better she liked him. The only explanation she could think of for her fondness was the fact that he was so similar to her in looks, and constantly reminded her of her dear departed papa.

She raised her whip and pointed. 'Once we turn into Bond Street, which is the next thoroughfare, it will be far more interesting and much quieter. We traverse from what is referred to as Old Bond Street into New Bond Street, and then will turn into Grosvenor Street which leads directly to our destination.'

He wasn't listening, but staring

across at two young ladies, correctly accompanied by their maidservants, strolling down the pavement.

'Good grief — those bonnets remind me of a coal scuttle — how in God's name can they see where they're going in such ridiculous hats?' She was about to reply when he turned and looked at her directly. His eyes were brimming with amusement. 'I forbid you to wear anything of that sort. I'm quite clear on that matter.'

She nodded. 'As always, your grace, I shall follow your instructions meticulously.' She sighed dramatically and shook her head as if sorely troubled. 'How will my sisters and I manage with no bonnets between us that will meet with your approval? I fear we must resort to borrowing Mama's turbans in order to be able to leave the house suitably accoutred.'

His sudden shout of laughter at her nonsense not only startled their horses but also attracted unwanted attention from those within earshot.

By the time they were both safely settled in their saddles they'd reached the turning that they required. Othello had never travelled with her to Town, so was unaware they were within half a mile of his new stable. The animals were flagging a bit after so long a journey, so they were obliged to remain at a sedate walk.

When they entered Grosvenor Square, she reined in to allow him to take in the magnificence of the central park which was at its very best in late spring.

'This is a splendid square, Amanda. No doubt each of the houses will be occupied by families here to launch a daughter or find a suitable bride for a son.'

'You might be surprised to know that not everyone is like us and prefers to remain in the country. Some actually enjoy attending prestigious events and having the opportunity to wear their new ensembles.'

'More fool them. I shall endure the

torture only for your sakes. How soon can we return to Suffolk? Do I have to remain the entire time, or can I leave you here unsupervised?'

'You must be here until Sarah has been introduced to all the important families — and, of course, for her own ball. After that, it will raise no eyebrows if you return home. No doubt you wish to oversee the demolition and laying of the foundations for the new Hall.'

'Exactly so.' He gestured towards the most magnificent of the edifices that surrounded Grosvenor Square. 'I must assume that one is now my property?'

'I'm sorry to disappoint you, but the Sinclair house is less ostentatious. It's the one adjacent to it.'

He chuckled. Their town house was only a smidgen smaller and equally grand.

'Then I'm suitably impressed. I take it we go in through the archway on the right?'

'The stables and coach houses are

obviously at the rear of the building. Only the houses on this side of the square have so much land. You will have noticed that along the other side the houses are joined. In order to reach the stabling for them, one has to go to the end of the row, and then make one's way back to whichever buildings belong to one's abode.'

'Fascinating, my dear, but I've no interest in the other side of the square.' He grinned. 'And very little interest in those adjacent to ours. I doubt I'll ever be comfortable owning so much when millions of folk are barely scraping a living.'

It was better to ignore his revolutionary comments and continue the discussion when they were in private. It wouldn't do for servants to overhear such things from the new duke.

'We can dismount here, directly outside; the grooms will take the horses around to the stables.'

An observant footman had alerted the butler and housekeeper, and the front door opened as if by magic. They were bowed in formally.

'I'll show you to your suite of rooms, Richard. Family chambers are on the first floor, and guests and so on are on the second. Staff have their accommodation in the attics.'

There were vases of flowers placed everywhere to welcome them, and the pleasing aroma spread throughout the vast entrance hall. Climbing the stairs was surprisingly difficult — she must be more fatigued than she had thought.

'This is the door to your drawing room — my mother has the apartment next to yours, and my sisters and I are across the passageway. Beth remains with us when we're here.'

★   ★   ★

After the comfortable size of the Dower House, Richard found Sinclair House alarmingly large. He got lost several times over the first few days, and had recourse to seek assistance from a lurking footman. He took the opportunity to visit both his own lawyer and the Sinclair lawyers. On both occasions he had O'Riley with him, and was confident his man would be able to deal with his legal matters unsupervised in future.

The ladies of the house were busy with feminine nonsense and he was happy to keep out of their way. He had an inherited membership to White's, and preferred to dine there rather than in Grosvenor Square, where he would be obliged to put on evening dress. If he arrived at his club in the afternoon and remained there, then not even the supercilious footmen queried his lack of dress. The duchess had decided that, as they were in Town, etiquette would be followed — that country ways were not acceptable now.

He and O'Riley were strolling along Bond Street when he spotted Miss Westley just ahead of them.

'It would appear that companions don't have to follow the same rules as the daughters of the *ton*.'

'It ain't — it *isn't* considered improper for young ladies of quality to walk along here without a chaperone, as long as they have a maid or footman in attendance.'

Richard raised an eyebrow. 'When did you become an expert on society manners?'

'Miss Westley has been explaining it to me. We often dine with the housekeeper and butler as neither of us like eating alone from a tray.'

'Remember, Patrick, you're not in a position to take on a wife.'

'Who said anything about wedlock, your grace? We just enjoy each other's company — nothing more.'

As their stride was longer, they were soon level with her. He wasn't sure he wanted to continue the journey if the two of them were to be looking soulfully into each other's eyes.

He greeted her politely, but then excused himself, saying he had business across the street. He dodged between the traffic and arrived safely on the other side. Once there he looked back, expecting to see the young woman hanging on to Patrick's arm. They were walking together but with at least a yard between them. Perhaps he had misjudged the situation.

As long as Patrick, who he considered to be a friend as well as an employee now, stayed clear of Horse Guards whilst in London, he thought he should be safe enough from detection.

Tonight was the first time he would be escorting his ladies to an event, and he was almost looking forward to seeing them dressed to impress. It was to be an informal supper party at the home of a Lord and Lady Forsyth who lived two houses from them. At least they wouldn't have to go there in a carriage. He would much prefer to put on his regimentals, but he no longer had the right to wear his uniform.

Beth was attempting to roll a hoop from one side to the other of the chequered entrance hall. He caught it as it was about to fall over, and with a smile bowled it back to her.

'Why does it wobble when I do it, Cousin Richard?'

'Perhaps you're not putting enough effort into the push. Show me how you do it. Send it to me.'

She tried, but again it failed to travel very far before falling over. He saw the danger signs and moved swiftly to avoid a tantrum. 'Let me help you, little one. I'll stand beside you and put my hands over yours and we can do it together.'

She skipped from one foot to the other in delight. 'Yes please. That would be lovely.'

'If we stand on this far corner and send it diagonally across the floor, it will have further to go and be able to travel faster.'

'What's diagonally?'

He demonstrated with his hand and she nodded. They got into position, and this time she put maximum effort into the push — as did he. To his horror, the metal hoop took off into the air and flew across the space before smashing through a window.

The resulting noise brought several footmen running, as well as the duchess and Amanda. 'Tarnation take it! That wasn't supposed to happen.'

Beth, instead of looking cowed and distressed by the disaster, was giggling helplessly. 'That was so funny. I didn't know you could throw a hoop out of the window like that.'

'Good heavens, this is all very unseemly. Elizabeth, you were told that you couldn't play with this inside, and were to take it out into the garden at the rear of the building. I'm most displeased with you.'

'Your grace, the accident is entirely my fault. I suggested we try and send it across the hall — but, as you can see, applied too much force.'

'That's as may be, sir, but my daughter knows she should not have had that object in here at all. Elizabeth, you will go back upstairs and remain

187

with your nanny until I give you leave to come down.'

'Cousin Richard, will you fetch my hoop for me, please? I shall need it to practice in the garden next time.' Then she ran lightly up the stairs, still giggling, and obviously unbothered by her set-down.

Amanda was examining the damage. 'I suppose there's nothing we can say to you about this. After all, if you wish to break windows that's your prerogative.'

'That's doing it too brown, my dear. I might be the duke, but I'm not an imbecile.' He wasn't sure if she was genuinely at odds with him or jesting. Not wishing to exacerbate the matter, he decided to take a neutral position. 'Someone could have been seriously injured by flying glass, and for that I apologise. It just didn't occur to me that bowling a hoop indoors was strictly forbidden.'

Her smile was tight, and he was relieved he hadn't made a humorous response. 'You're excused this time, your grace. As you've had no interaction with children, one cannot expect you to understand the rules.' He was about to agree, but she continued, 'However, one would have thought that any man of sense, whether familiar with children or not, would realise a metal hoop is not something to be played with in the house.'

She'd addressed him as if he was an unruly schoolboy. All desire to laugh evaporated. No one — not even Lady Amanda Sinclair — could be allowed to speak to him like that and escape unscathed.

'Might I remind you, miss, to whom you are speaking? I am your guardian, and will be spoken to with respect at all times. Do I make myself quite clear?'

His tone was clipped and his expression arctic. It had the desired effect, and immediately she curtsied.

'I apologise, your grace, if I inadvertently offended you. Pray excuse me, I must return to my apartment.'

For the first time since he'd met

her, her limp was noticeable, and he cursed his maladroit and heavy-handed response. She was halfway up the stairs when he bounded after her and arrived at her side before she reached the top.

'Amanda, please wait. That was unforgivable of me. I forget that I'm not an officer speaking to my subordinates, and treated you abominably.'

She kept her face averted and mumbled something he couldn't make out clearly. He was a brute and had made her weep. He delved into his waistcoat, pulled out a pristine hand-kerchief and pushed it into her unresisting fingers.

'Dry your eyes, sweetheart . . .'

For some reason, this last remark elicited a response, but not the one he wished for or expected.

★　★　★

Her distress was quashed by her anger at his casual use of an endearment best

190

used to a small child or one's beloved. She was neither.

She glared at him and was delighted that he recoiled from her. 'I thank you, your grace, to desist from using such unsuitable terms when addressing me. Keep them for Beth in future.' She tossed his unused handkerchief back in his face, which was hardly polite or the action of a mature young lady.

She'd barely reached the top stair when he was in front of her. He was a formidable figure, and even more so when angry. But for some reason she wasn't worried that he would physically chastise her. He might bark, shout and give her an almighty set-down, but she was absolutely certain he'd never raise a hand to her.

Her intention had been to apologise again for her childish behaviour and insolence, and this time make sure he understood she was sincere. Her mouth opened, but the words that came out were quite different to those she'd been thinking. Even worse, her hands, of their own volition, came up to rest on his impressive chest.

'Did you know your eyes turn from pale to dark, to the shade of an emerald, when you're enraged?'

He reached out and took her hands in his and gently removed them from his person. 'I think, my dear girl, that is an irrelevant but interesting fact. I am torn between two actions — one to put you across my knee and administer a well-deserved spanking . . . '

He paused, and for a terrifying second, she thought she'd been mistaken in her assessment of his character.

' . . . or take you in my arms and kiss you. Which would you prefer?'

Her cheeks were hot, but from somewhere she found the resolve to answer him without revealing her true feelings. 'As I've not experienced either, I cannot honestly give you an opinion on the matter.'

The tension between them melted

192

like snow in summer sunshine. 'Good God! I can't believe you think that being kissed by me will be a similar experience to being put across my knee. I can assure you, the first you would enjoy, and the second not at all.' His smile was wicked; she belatedly recognised his intent and moved too late. She was trapped against the wall as he put an arm on either side of her.

He gave her no opportunity to protest. He lowered his head and his lips covered hers. She was too shocked to struggle. Then an unexpected heat spread around her body like wildfire, and instead of pushing him away she leaned into his embrace. His arms encircled her and she was lifted from her feet. His mouth moved across hers, and if she hadn't been in mid-air her legs would have given way at the sheer pleasure of it.

Her fingers became embedded in the hair at the back of his neck. Every inch of her was pressed against him. She was lost to all sense.

Then he put her aside as if she was red-hot. Had she done something to offend him by her wanton behaviour?

'That was unpardonable. I took shameful advantage of you. I will speak to your mother immediately and ask for her permission . . .'

Sanity returned. Hearing his words had the same effect as being doused with a bucket of icy water. 'You'll do no such thing, Richard. We exchanged a kiss, and most enjoyable it was too. I don't consider myself compromised, as only the two of us are aware of what took place. Becoming betrothed to you would be completely inappropriate and quite unacceptable.'

The hectic colour along his cheekbones was fading, and he was listening carefully to what she said.

'Forgive me if you think I'm being patronising, but I don't believe that you're aware that for a guardian to marry his ward would create a scandal that this family might never recover from. Not only am I your ward, we're also related — however distantly it might be.'

He looked baffled by her statement and ran his hands through his hair, making it unruly, and she wanted to reach out and smooth it down for him.

'That's nonsense and you know it. The connection between us by blood is so tenuous as to be almost non-existent. You will reach your majority later this year and will be no longer be under my command.'

'Command?'

'Yes — I prefer it to the alternative. However, if you don't consider that I need to marry you, then I'll accept your decision.' His smile appeared sad. 'I thought you told me I was the most eligible parti in the land? Now I'm crushed that you've rejected me.'

Fortunately, she realised he was funning before she said something foolish. 'A man with an ego as large as yours will soon recover.' She moved away from him towards her apartment — talking to him whilst in such close proximity was giving her palpitations. 'Anyway, admit that you're relieved you don't have to marry a plain beanpole of a girl with a disfigurement.'

# 11

Richard wasn't impressed with his behaviour. He'd been a respected and fierce officer, but always fair — why in hell's name was he behaving this way? First he'd berated Amanda unnecessarily, and then he'd kissed her. He was deeply ashamed that he'd violated the trust between a person *in loco parentis* and his ward.

Tonight, he donned his hated evening black without complaint. When his valet smoothed his jacket over his shoulders it reminded him of the soft touch of her fingers when she'd put them in his hair.

'That's enough. It'll do. Don't wait up.'

Beth had already retired, as she was still in disgrace for her disobedience. Although she had only the intelligence of a six-year-old, she was perfectly capable of understanding an instruction. Therefore, he had been duped by a child, and this too was out of character.

He slumped in a chair in the drawing room whilst he waited for the ladies to appear in their finery. He heard voices approaching the staircase, and moved to a position where he could watch them descending without being seen himself.

The dowager sailed ahead, the feathers in her turban waving wildly as she descended. Her gown was burgundy tonight, as was her entire ensemble.

Sarah followed, wearing a delightful confection in pale blue with a dark blue sash and embroidery. He would have to be vigilant if he was to keep her safe from predatory suitors. She looked quite beautiful.

'Where's Amanda?' He hadn't intended to sound so abrupt, but was concerned that she hadn't come down.

'My oldest daughter is indisposed, your grace; she sends her apologies.'

He ignored this explanation, stepped around the speaker, and went in search of the missing girl. She'd been perfectly well an hour ago, and the only explanation was that she was overset by what had taken place between them.

He knocked loudly on her sitting-room door and waited to be invited in. No one answered so he went in anyway.

There was movement behind the closed door to the right, so Amanda must be in there. This time he didn't bother to knock, knowing he'd get no response.

'Amanda, if you don't come downstairs immediately then no one will be going to the party. Do you wish to deny your mother and your sister the pleasure of their first London event?'

This was hardly fair, but he could think of no other incentive to get her to change her mind. The door was opened, not by her, but by a trembling maid.

'I beg your pardon, your grace, but Lady Amanda isn't here.'

'Then where the devil is she?'

'I don't know. I went to fetch the hot water, and when I got back she was gone.'

'What was she wearing? Had she changed her clothes?'

The girl had the sense to check the closet before answering, and reappeared looking puzzled. 'Her riding habit is missing, your grace.'

His language made her flinch. His wretched cousin had gone out on her stallion and it would be dark in an hour. For a young lady to ride in the park so late, even with a groom in attendance, wasn't sensible or safe.

Ignoring common sense and etiquette, he ran to the gallery and yelled down to the ladies waiting below, 'Amanda's gone out on her horse alone. I must go after her. Go ahead of us and we'll join you as soon as we can.'

It was hard to tell whether the two of them were more shocked by his parade-ground voice, or the fact that Amanda had done something so idiotic.

The duchess recovered her aplomb. 'There is no need to shout in that unseemly fashion, young man. Sarah and I will wait until you and my errant daughter are ready to accompany us.'

This time he replied in a more moderate tone. 'You will not. It would be the height of rudeness for all of us to be late. You will have two footmen accompanying you, and I'm certain you'll come to no harm walking one hundred yards across the square without me at your side.'

He'd given a direct order, and whatever her personal opinion on the subject, she had no option but to obey. Her basilisk stare might have quelled a less hardy gentleman. He bowed and raced to his apartment.

'Riding gear — now — and send word to the stables to have my gelding saddled.'

The nights were lighter now but the sun had set, and there could be any number of miscreants, footpads or murderers lurking in the undergrowth of both Hyde and Green Parks.

He took the backstairs and thundered down, making the candles in the wall sconces flicker as he rushed past. Fortunately for the stable hands his horse was waiting, as were two grooms. They both had lanterns dangling from poles, but these were, as yet, unlit.

'Your grace, I heard that Lady Amanda's missing. I have my pistol and my sword. I think it best at least one of us is armed.'

'Good man, O'Riley. I might have known you'd be waiting for me. How long has she been gone?' he asked as he swung into the saddle.

'According to the head groom, about half an hour. She's taken one man with her, so is not entirely alone.' If he hadn't known that his man was Irish, he would have thought him an English gentleman born and bred in this country.

It was but few hundred yards down Upper Grosvenor Street to Park Lane, which encircled the open land. They clattered through at a spanking trot — he would have preferred to gallop, but didn't want to draw attention to the fact that they were going in search of a missing young lady.

As they entered the gates, he dug his heels in, and his mount responded by breaking instantly into a canter. There were acres and acres of land to search if she'd been foolish enough to leave the main thoroughfare. He pointed with his whip to where the track divided just ahead. 'Take one of the men and search to the left; I'll take the other and go right.'

He stood in his stirrups in order to get a better view, as the track dipped and he couldn't see into the hollow. This was deserted — in fact, they'd only passed a handful of riders, no pedestrians at all, and one carriage.

Those that used the park did so in the afternoon. Anyone of sense would now be sitting down to dine in the comfort of their own home. Or, like his own family, setting out for some sort of social event.

What had possessed her to go out at such an hour? As far as he was aware, she'd visited London many times with the old duke, and would know how things went on here. There was no excuse whatsoever for such foolhardy behaviour, and when he had her home he would tell her so in no uncertain terms.

★ ★ ★

Amanda had been so lost in her own thoughts that she had paid little attention to what was going on around her. Then, after she'd been cantering down the path in the park for a mile or two, she became aware that she was the only rider still out.

Only then did she consider the implications of rushing off like this at such an hour. After her disturbing meeting with Richard, she'd been too restless to remain indoors. She'd sent a message with Mary to her mother, pleading a megrim. No one would disturb her if they thought her unwell with one of her occasional unpleasant sick headaches.

She thanked the good Lord that Richard would never hear of her rash behaviour. He might not be well versed in the etiquette of society, but would be aware that no young lady of sense would venture out at such a time.

She drew rein and allowed her groom to come alongside. 'Tom, I think we should return home immediately. I've no wish to be out here in the dark, especially as we have no lantern with us.'

The look of relief on his face was quite comical. 'I know a shortcut, my lady; if we take that, we'll be back in half the time.'

There was a myriad of small paths and tracks leading from the main well-travelled one. She wouldn't dream of venturing here without a guide, but as Tom knew the route, she would follow him. The sooner she was home and safely in bed, the happier she'd be.

The route they took brought them out opposite the entrance to Mount Street, and from here it was only five minutes to the house. She dismounted before they reached the stable yard, slipped inside through the side door, and hurried upstairs.

She'd dismissed her maid earlier, so was unsurprised to find her apartment empty. She quickly stripped off her riding habit and carefully folded it back onto the shelf in the closet, completed her ablutions, pulled on her nightgown and scrambled into bed. She then drew the curtains around the four-poster and flopped back on the pillows.

Her heart was hammering. It would serve her right if she did now get a megrim. The excitement, anxiety and exercise were enough to send her immediately into a deep, dreamless sleep.

★ ★ ★

Richard had been searching fruitlessly for two hours when he was hailed by a rider galloping towards him. His heart plummeted to his boots. He urged his horse forward, dreading to hear what might have brought the groom at such a pace.

'Your grace, your grace, Lady Amanda's stallion's back in the stables.'

'Thank you — we'll return at once.'

This time he disregarded the startled glances of those strolling to their evening entertainment, and continued at a gallop down the street and into the square.

He tossed his reins to a waiting groom and rushed upstairs. He burst into her apartment. Her maid was sitting by the fire mending stockings in the sitting room, and squealed with shock at his sudden entrance.

'How long has Lady Amanda been home?'

'She's not back, your grace. I've not seen her.' The girl wrung her hands and buried her face in her apron, crying noisily.

He'd no time for her histrionics. He looked into the bedchamber. It was dark, silent, the curtains drawn at the window and around the bed as before.

He turned and raced back to the stables. He should have spoken to someone there before he'd hurtled inside. If this had been a battle, his lack of direction would already have lost it.

The head groom appeared at his shout. 'I want to speak to the groom who took care of the stallion.'

'That would be Tom, your grace; he went for supper after he'd taken care of both horses.'

Richard's head began to clear. He'd thought Othello had returned riderless, but this was obviously not the case.

There was only one explanation — Amanda had changed from her habit into her evening gown and taken herself off to the party. This time, he wouldn't charge after her until he'd made absolutely certain this was what had actually happened.

He strode into her apartment only to

find that the maid was no longer there. The bedchamber was still silent. He swore long and loud.

His feet left the ground when the missing girl spoke to him from the darkness.

'Richard, don't use such language in my bedroom. What are you doing in here, anyway?'

In two strides he reached the bed and grabbed the curtains so fiercely they tore from the poles.

'God's teeth, woman, don't you know that I've spent the past three hours searching for you in the park whilst you've been sleeping peacefully in your bed?'

'Of course I didn't know; what a stupid question. You've ruined my bed, and you shouldn't be in here anyway. If you continue to behave in this fashion, you'll find yourself saddled with me whether you like it or not. Go away — I'll speak to you in the morning.'

His eyes had adjusted to the darkness and he could now see her shape under the covers. It took him several steadying breaths to recover his temper before he did something they'd both regret.

'It's too late for me to attend the event to which I agreed to go. There will be a reckoning tomorrow, my girl. Present yourself in the library at eight o'clock. Do I make myself quite clear?'

'You do, sir.'

Her response was so quiet he only just heard it. He closed the door with remarkable restraint and headed for the library. On the way he ordered a jug of coffee, a decanter of brandy and whatever was available in the kitchen.

By the time the trays arrived he'd scribbled a note to be delivered to the duchess. In this he apologised for Amanda's and his absence, and promised to explain the reason in the morning.

As far as he knew, this sort of event didn't go on into the small hours, so they would be home shortly. He had no wish to speak to them tonight. He was on his second sandwich and third coffee before he recalled exactly what Amanda had said before he'd snarled at her.

He choked on his mouthful, and was on his feet and moving towards the door before he stopped coughing. His boots were leaning drunkenly against the edge of his chair and he was in his stockings. He didn't pause to put them on. After grabbing a candle, he headed for the backstairs for the second time that night.

This time he went to the door that led directly to her bedchamber, and quietly opened it and stepped in. The single flame was sufficient for him to see her huddled shape in the ruined bed.

He lit four more candles before moving closer. From the stillness of the shape under the covers he knew she was awake.

'Amanda, forgive me for disturbing you again. We need to talk — not tomorrow, but tonight.'

'Go away, I'm asleep.'

His lips twitched, and he spun a hard-back chair and straddled it. 'I wasn't listening to you when I was here earlier — I was too incensed. I'd been beside myself with worry that you'd met with some disaster, had been abducted or worse. My relief at finding you safe in bed made me speak so violently.'

She shifted slightly but didn't sit up or respond. He knew she was listening.

'I was eating my supper . . . '

This comment elicited her sudden appearance from beneath the sheets. 'How dare you come in here and talk about food when I'm dying of starvation and cannot sleep because of it.'

Her glorious hair was tumbling around her shoulders, her stunning eyes were vivid in her face — no woman had never looked more beautiful to him.

Only then did it become clear to him. His irrational behaviour and lack of clarity these past weeks was caused by her. Some quirk of fate had thrown them together: now he was hopelessly in love with her, and she was unavailable to him.

Why was he staring at her as if seeing her for the first time? What had really brought him here?

'Richard, I really am sorry I caused you so much aggravation. But you must go at once; it's quite beyond the pale for you to be in here when I'm in bed.'

Instead of leaping to his feet and retreating, he remained where he was with his head resting on his hands, and smiled. 'You forgot to mention, sweetheart, that I'm bootless.' He nodded towards his stockings and her eyes widened.

'How extraordinary! But you really must go, and we will talk in the morning.' Her stomach gurgled loudly, and the strange tension that had been crackling in the air dissipated when he chuckled.

'Get dressed. You need to eat, and we need to talk. I'll order more food to be sent to the library.' He rose in one smooth motion, picked up the chair one-handed and replaced it in the corner. Then, with a casual wave, he padded out, leaving her in turmoil.

The lure of food, however, was enough to get her out of bed and into her closet. She snatched up a handful of undergarments and a gown she knew would drop over her head without the help of her maid.

In less than ten minutes she was decent — no stockings, and bare feet, but everything else in place. She'd hastily plaited her hair, but it was left dangling in one long braid between her shoulders.

Her sister and mother would be returning in an hour or so — this clandestine rendezvous must be finished before then. However innocent, it would be difficult to explain to anyone else.

Despite the swiftness of her appearance there was already a sumptuous spread set out on the central table. More than enough for half a dozen, let alone the two of them. The delicious smell of freshly brewed coffee wafted across the room, making her mouth water.

He was standing, his boots securely on his feet — thank goodness — poised to serve her.

Eating was more important than talking, and between them they ate more than they should before they were satiated. She was the first to drop her cutlery.

'I'm replete — but I'd like some more coffee if there is any.'

He hefted the silver pot and shook his head sadly. Then he grinned, making him look years younger and far more attractive. The door had been left wide open, and a footman walked in carrying a second jug without having been sent for.

'Put it there. I require nothing further; thank you for your assistance tonight.'

The young man smiled and bowed. 'Yes, your grace. I was told to inform you that her grace and Lady Sarah have safely returned and are now upstairs. The house is locked for the night.'

'Excellent. This can be cleared in the morning. Tell the staff they may retire.'

Once they were private again, he refilled her cup. She stood up and tipped a generous measure of brandy into it, and couldn't restrain her gurgle of laughter at his shock.

'Don't look so curmudgeonly, Richard, I've been drinking alcohol since my come-out two years ago. I didn't have a Season as I broke my leg the year I was to come here. Then my dearest papa died, and all thought of it was forgotten.'

'You never take wine at dinner, so I didn't know that you liked strong liquor.'

'Hardly that. I don't like wine, but I do enjoy a glass or two of champagne when it's offered. Papa introduced me to cognac, but not neat, only in my chocolate or coffee.'

He poured himself a large glass and sipped it. 'This is excellent — far too good to be wasted in that way.'

'Then I suggest in future you ask for an inferior one to be served to me.' She put her cup on the table. 'Why did you come to my room? When you left, you were so angry I was terrified. Yet half an hour later you returned quite differently.'

# 12

Richard had been dreading this question. How was he to explain to her the reason for his mercurial behaviour without revealing his true feelings? Then his world righted. Had it not been she who had said he could be saddled with her? She must believe it would be possible for them to marry. He would tread carefully — not alarm her — she was an innocent, and he'd no wish to make her feel obligated to accept his offer because of his behaviour.

'It was your derogatory comment about yourself that brought me back. It would be an honour for myself or any other gentleman to have you as their bride. You're a lovely young lady in every respect, and your limp is scarcely noticeable . . . '

Her smile faded. Before he could prevent it, she leaned down and pulled up her skirts, revealing the true extent of her injury.

'See, my limp might be almost imperceptible, but the scar on my leg is quite hideous.'

He wasn't sure if he should be shocked by her improper behaviour, or concerned that she obviously thought of him as an older brother, and not a potential husband, or she wouldn't have shown her bare leg to him.

His instinct to protect overcame his scruples, and he knelt beside her and put her leg on his thigh. He ran his fingers from just above the knee to her ankle, tracing the line of the scar. He wanted to kiss every inch of it; but, more dangerously, he wanted to pull her down onto his lap and make love to her. Why hadn't she put on stockings and shoes before coming down?

He replaced her foot and flicked down her skirts before standing.

'It's not pretty, but not as bad as you think. If I was considering you as a bride, it certainly wouldn't put me off.'

He turned and flicked his coat over his embarrassment, and fussed with the coffee pot until it was safe to resume his seat.

'Anyway, Richard, now I come to think of it, by the time any husband saw how bad it was, it would be too late to recant as we would be married.'

Her words were like a hammer blow to his heart. He was about to say something that would reveal his intentions, but she spoke again.

'The question is academic as I've no intention of marrying anyone. My parents were supposedly well-matched, but barely spoke, and certainly slept in separate chambers for as long as I can remember. I intend to remain at home and take care of my sister, and be a devoted aunt to any children that Sarah might have.'

'And a perfectly splendid aunt you will make. Forgive me for saying so, my dear, but might I respectfully suggest that you refrain from showing your naked limbs to any other gentleman?'

He'd expected her to be flustered by his drawing attention to her immodest action, but instead she smiled widely.

'You're a nincompoop, cousin, to think I'd show anyone else but you. I consider you as my older brother, as you very well know. Which brings us to the other thing that we're both tiptoeing around.'

'The fact that I kissed you? Or that you suggested I might be forced to offer for you after visiting you in your bedchamber?'

'Yes, both of those are pertinent. There appears to be a blurring of lines between us. I've thought about it carefully, and decided I prefer to think of you in the role of sibling rather than potential suitor. Therefore, although I did enjoy being kissed by you, it would be most improper for it to happen again. Siblings absolutely don't exchange that sort of kiss.'

'I'm mortally offended that you don't consider I'd make you a suitable husband.' He clutched his chest in a parody of a broken-hearted lover and, as he'd hoped, she laughed at his tomfoolery. 'I'll remain forever a bachelor nursing my wounded pride.'

'You'll do no such thing, Richard. I told you that I intend to find you someone you can be comfortable with whilst we're here. Unfortunately, I missed my first opportunity by dashing off in that ridiculous fashion.'

'Then I'll make it my business to find *you* someone that you would be happy with. It's hardly fair for you to have all the fun.'

'I accept the challenge. We'll reconvene tomorrow morning, and present each other with a list of requirements so there can be no confusion as to the sort of person we're looking for.'

'I think that first we must both eat humble pie with your mama. I doubt that she'll be happy about our non-appearance.'

'Does she have to know what actually happened?'

'She already does know that you went

out on your horse, so that bird has flown.'

'I'm too fatigued to think of anything right now. You're always telling us that you were an officer, a military gentleman — surely it's for you to come up with a solution, not for an unworldly young lady such as myself?'

'Go to bed, you unprincipled baggage, I can see you intend to run me ragged before we return to the safety of our country estate.'

Despite her infirmity she moved with grace — in fact, everything about her was perfect. She paused at the door and her smile made her look even more beautiful in his opinion.

'I love it that you refer to Denchester Hall as *ours*, rather than *yours*. I've decided that when the new building's complete I'd like to move in there with you.'

'I can assure you, my dear girl, that I always intended that you should.'

He drained the last of the coffee and sank most of the decanter before following her example. He wasn't quite sure how he felt. He was in love for the first time in his life, and that was something to be joyful about. However, persuading his darling girl that he wasn't her brother, but a potential lover, was going to be difficult.

More pressing was what excuse he could present to the duchess in the morning that wouldn't exacerbate matters. Amanda was correct to suggest he should be able to do this, but lately he hadn't been able to marshal his thoughts as he had in the army. Was he becoming soft after so short a time as a civilian?

★ ★ ★

Amanda woke early, eager to get on with the business of writing her list of requirements to give to Richard. She intended to make it both comprehensive and impossible to fulfil. She sat at her escritoire and compiled the list. The more she wrote, the more she warmed to the task.

Two yards tall in stockinged feet.
Broad-shouldered and athletic
 build.
No more than thirty years of age.
Clean-shaven.
Abundant hair on head — colour
 immaterial.
Colour of eyes unimportant, but
 must be set apart and not small.
Regular features.
Full set of undamaged teeth.
An earl at the least.
Not been married before.
Intelligent and with a good sense
 of humour.
No interest in blood sports, gam-
 bling or heavy drinking.
No interfering mother.
Prefers to live in the countryside.
Does not require me to gallivant
 all over the country with him
 visiting relatives and friends.
An interest in breeding horses and
 dogs.

*An excellent landlord to his ten-
ants and a good employer to his
staff.*

She read it through and was laughing
by the end. If such a paragon existed,
the likelihood of him being found was
almost nil.

Mary came in with her chocolate, but
she waved it aside. 'Find me something
pretty to wear, please, preferably a new
gown.'

The girl appeared with three and laid
them across the end of the bed. 'The
daffodil yellow with the golden sash is
very attractive, my lady. Or the
duck-egg blue with the turquoise
beading.' She picked up the third.
'Perhaps you would prefer the green
sprig muslin with the emerald sash and
embroidery?'

'The sprig muslin, Mary. I also wish
to have my hair dressed more elabo-
rately, but I'm in a desperate hurry as
I'm to meet his grace in the library at
eight o'clock, and I do so wish to have

my breakfast first.'

'I've been practising a new style, my lady, and I think it would take less time than your usual coronet.'

Her hair was put up in an attractive coil at the back of her head, leaving curls escaping on either side of her face. Normally she had it plaited and pinned tightly around her head — this really was a great improvement.

The gown was equally fetching; her eyes sparkled and her cheeks were flushed with excitement. One might almost think one was attractive when dressed in such an ensemble.

'Here you are, my lady, just the matching slippers and reticule. If you intend to go walking there are boots, bonnet and spencer made to complement this gown.'

'Thank you, Mary, you have worked a miracle today.'

The tall-case clock that stood proudly against the wall of the entrance hall struck eight as she dashed past. Her mother never rose before midday, but her sister was often down early. Richard had usually broken his fast and gone about his business before either of them arrived. She hoped this was the case this morning.

The breakfast room was empty, but the usual tempting array of dishes stood in their silver-lidded dishes on the sideboard. The footman was waiting to offer his assistance if needed. He knew that she preferred coffee and Mama and Sarah took tea.

With a piled plate she headed for the table, the list for Richard burning a hole in her pocket. 'Has his grace eaten yet?'

'No, not this morning, my lady.'

She poured herself some of the dark, aromatic brew she loved, and proceeded to demolish her substantial breakfast. She was fortunate indeed that whatever she ate she remained slender — but today she was wearing a gown that showed off her feminine curves to perfection. She wanted him to know that, despite her lack of substance, she was every inch a woman grown.

The only reason she wished him to know this, of course, was so that he could be sure she wouldn't disappoint her mythical future husband.

Her empty plate had vanished and been replaced by a fresh one, on which she had two slices of toast and marmalade, when he sauntered in looking immaculate in his dark-blue topcoat, grey silk waistcoat and snowy cravat.

'Good morning, Amanda. Might I be permitted to compliment you on your appearance? I'm not exactly sure whether a sibling would even notice what his sister was wearing. But I'm not blind to the fact that you're wearing a new ensemble, and it behoves me to acknowledge this fact.'

She stood up and slowly turned around so he could get an uninterrupted view of her splendid outfit. 'I put this on especially so you would know exactly how to describe me to my possible suitors.' This was the perfect time to hand him her list. 'There you are, these are my exact requirements, and nothing else will do.' She held her hand out imperiously, and he placed a similar item on her palm.

'And these are mine. I thought you might like to know that I decided, as I'm the Duke of Denchester, I've no need to explain anything to your mother or anyone else about last night. I shall just apologise politely for being absent.'

She resumed her seat and he joined her once he had selected his breakfast. A fresh pot of coffee appeared without being requested. Should she look at his list when he was present, or wait until she was alone? Whatever he did, she would do the same.

He put her list on the table beside his plate, but made no attempt to open it. She fidgeted and then, unable to contain her impatience, stood up abruptly. 'I intend to go shopping in Bond Street later; do I have your permission to do so?'

His laden fork was poised in front of his mouth, and with a sigh of resignation he replaced it on his plate. 'I think, my dear girl, that what you should have said is this: 'Do I have your permission to go to Bond Street, as I would dearly like to do so?' Not tell me what you are going to do, and then belatedly ask if you're allowed to do so.'

'Semantics, my dear Richard, and well you know it. As you so rightly pointed out the other day, I'll be one-and-twenty in three months, and can then do exactly as I please.'

'I think you will find that until you're married you remain my responsibility. Do you wish to have a grand ball to celebrate your anniversary?'

'Absolutely not. Even if I wanted to, it would be impossible: the Dower House can only accommodate fifty people at the most, and the Hall will be in ruins by then.'

★ ★ ★

'Then we shall have marquees in the grounds. I insist that we invite the entire neighbourhood and make it a double celebration. I've yet to meet my neighbours or many of my tenants, or those that reside in my villages. We can have a garden party in the afternoon, and invite staff and similar folk in the evening for a ball for your name day.'

He sincerely hoped it would be their nuptials they would be celebrating as well as her anniversary.

'As you please, your grace; after all, I am entirely under your control. When I'm five-and-thirty, you might have tired of dictating how I live my life — at least, I hope so.'

He hid his smile in his napkin. By the time she was that age, they would have been married for years and hopefully have a nursery full of children who looked exactly like her. She might not realise it, but he was her perfect man, and he was damned if any nonsense about etiquette would come between him and the woman he was besotted with. As his wife she would still be legally his to command, but he would never rein in her wild spirit or her energy for life.

'There's no necessity for me to answer that question, as by then you will be happily married and surrounded by children and a devoted husband.'

'Of course, as will you. How happy we both shall be, living in our separate establishments and no longer associating in this irritating fashion every moment of the day.'

She dropped her napkin on her empty plate. Her smile was somewhat forced, but he nodded as if he hadn't noticed. 'I'll peruse your list when I get a moment. If I remember correctly, we remain at home this evening, so I'll dine at my club.'

As soon as she'd left the room, he opened the list and scanned the contents. By the end he was laughing openly. She might not realise it, but he fitted every one of those requirements perfectly. Would she recognise herself in his list?

\* \* \*

He was damned if he was going to kick his heels all morning awaiting the arrival of the duchess although he'd better not offend her as she would, if he had his way, be his mother-in-law by the end of the summer. He didn't doubt for one minute that eventually Amanda would recognise she loved him as much as he loved her, and put aside her qualms.

If she didn't do it willingly, then he would contrive to so thoroughly compromise her she had no option but to concur. When they were safely married, she would soon understand this was how things were meant to be.

He quickly scribbled a note of apology to the duchess and left it with the butler.

O'Riley knocked on the library door, and he bid him enter. 'What can I do for you this morning?'

'Well, your grace, it's a touch sensitive. I attended the party last night as you instructed, and kept an eye on Lady Sarah.'

'Did something happen? Should I be concerned?'

'Not about the young lady, your grace — it's the duchess. She spent every moment playing cards, and by my reckoning lost several hundred pounds. She's a hardened gambler.'

'God's teeth! Then who was taking care of the girl?'

'Nothing to worry about on that score, your grace; Miss Westley never left her side. Lady Sarah behaved perfectly, and didn't dance with any gentleman more than once. She was properly introduced by the hostess, so I reckon all of them were acceptable.'

'Did she seem partial to any of those she partnered?'

'No, your grace, she just enjoyed the dancing and the company.'

Richard gestured that Patrick should take a seat. 'This business with the duchess is more serious. She insists on playing cards after dinner if I'm present, which is one reason why I absent myself as often as possible.'

'She was playing with other ladies, no gentleman at their table. Those seated with her changed several times, apart from two of them who had attended this event solely to gamble. They'd not come to dance, socialise or anything else. I regret to tell you that her grace was one of these.'

'And the other woman? Was she the one who gained from her grace's losses?'

'Not entirely, although she took a goodly amount; two others, who didn't stay the entire evening, also took a share of the winnings.'

'I need you to attend every event in future as well as Miss Westley. You must discover who her grace gambles with, and then investigate their provenance. It's perfectly possible that the duchess was dealt a series of bad hands and that is why she lost so heavily. She is certainly a lady who likes the thrill of risking her money. God knows, she has plenty of it to lose.'

'Are you considering that there might

be more to this? That the ladies who won have set out to fleece her?'

'I'm probably overcautious — but I've seen it happen. I've played often enough with the duchess to know that she's sharp-witted and an excellent card player. I imagine that it's unusual for her to lose so heavily.'

They sat in silence for a moment, both cogitating this disturbing news. 'Perhaps I'm worrying unnecessarily. In my experience, if someone was cheating in order to win, they would allow the person they'd targeted to win the first time they met. The fact that she lost is reassuring in some perverse way, and indicates that this is probably perfectly innocent.'

'I reckon it's worth keeping an eye on, nevertheless, your grace.'

'Absolutely. Was there anything else?' His man shook his head as he got to his feet. 'Then, my friend, you're free for the rest of the day. Just make sure I know where you are in case I need you.'

He recovered his note to the duchess

and decided he would speak to her in person. Not to apologise, but to warn her about her card playing.

# 13

Beth pleaded to be allowed to accompany Amanda and Sarah on their shopping expedition. 'Please, please, take me. I promise I'll be a good girl; I won't make a fuss, I'll walk quietly and pretend I'm a grown-up person.'

Miss Westley overheard this request. 'I'm not required by her grace until midday, my lady, so I'd be happy to accompany you and walk with Lady Elizabeth.'

'That would be splendid, if you're quite sure. Beth's always on her best behaviour with anyone else.' Amanda turned to her younger sister, who was skipping from foot to foot in excitement. 'You must go upstairs quietly and ask Nanny to get you ready. Be down here in one quarter of an hour. Can you do that, Beth?'

'I can, I can. I'll wear my new bonnet

and then I'll look ever so grown-up.'

She scampered off, followed closely by the maid who worked with Nanny to keep their sister safe and happy.

★ ★ ★

The short walk to Bond Street was accomplished without incident. All three of them were looking smart as paint, and it was quite obvious that Miss Westley was turning several heads as well.

'Beth's behaving perfectly, I'm so glad that Miss Westley agreed to return to us. I've asked her to become a permanent part of the family — I hope that meets with your approval, Sarah?'

'I was going to suggest that you did so. Do you not have to ask for either Richard or our mama's consent first?'

'I suppose I should have done, but too late to repine. The matter's settled. When Mama's companion returns next week, Miss Westley will become our companion and chaperone. From what

240

you've told me, you would have been in a sad case if she'd not stepped in last night to take the role that should have been filled by our mother.'

'Do you think that Mama's gambling is getting out of hand? I overheard two ladies saying she lost a lot of money last night.'

'I'll speak to Richard later — he'll have to deal with it, as he controls the purse strings now.'

Miss Westley and Beth had stopped to look at a particularly fine display of bonnets in a milliner's window, and were now several yards behind them.

Amanda touched Sarah's elbow. 'We'd better wait for them to catch up. I don't like Beth to be out without us close by.'

As she watched, two gentlemen stepped out of another emporium, and immediately stopped and bowed to Beth. It was obvious they'd mistaken her for Sarah.

It was impossible to hear what was said from that distance, but Beth's companion dealt with the matter efficiently. Amanda watched Beth curtsy politely; the two men bowed again, and then strode off in the opposite direction.

Her sister was about to pick up her skirts and race along the street, but her companion gently restrained her, and they walked sedately towards them.

'Sarah, those gentlemen thought I was you. I didn't tell them who I was, and they went away content. Are they friends of yours?'

'No, sweetheart, they're acquaintances only. I met them last night and I think I danced with the taller of the two — the one with the bright blue topcoat.'

Beth took her sister's hand and they hurried off, eager to get home and explain to their mama about the confusion.

'Thank you, Miss Westley, for managing the situation so well. It's exactly what I feared would happen if we brought Beth to Town.'

'I'm certain they didn't know they were speaking to anyone but Lady Sarah. Lady Elizabeth said nothing, merely smiled prettily and curtsied at exactly the right time. They were both popinjays, gentlemen of no account, not anyone that her ladyship should encourage.'

'Anyone who wears a coat of such a startling blue must be touched in the attic. We must all be vigilant that Beth doesn't come to grief, as she could easily be enticed away if an unscrupulous gentleman got the opportunity.'

'Oh, do not say so, my lady. If her grace will allow me, I'll move into the role of governess to your sister. I think that would be perfectly acceptable and suit the circumstances.'

'Miss Bennett will be back at any time to resume her duties as companion and secretary to my mother, so I'll take it upon myself to give you permission to become Beth's governess. There's much she can learn about behaving like a young lady. Despite her disability, she's the equivalent of a very intelligent child.'

On her arrival at the front door she was met by Sarah. 'I beg you, go to Mama. She's beside herself. Quite incoherent and unable to explain exactly what has happened. All I can glean is that Richard is to blame for her distress.'

Amanda quickly explained the new appointment, and Sarah made a hasty retreat, not wishing to be involved in any drama or unpleasantness herself.

She found her parent in the small drawing room at the rear of the house that overlooked the garden. She'd expected her to be in tears from what she'd been told, but instead her mother was pacing the room her face twisted with fury.

'Mama, whatever has upset you? Can I help in anyway?'

'Upset? I'm not upset, I'm angry with that man. How dare he have the impudence to tell me how to behave? He knows nothing about my life and that of others in our strata of society.'

'I'm afraid that it doesn't matter what he knows or where he came from, Mama, he is the duke and holds our lives in his hands. If you anger him, he could send you to live in Northumbria or Scotland — is that what you want to happen?'

Her mother deflated like a spent balloon. She collapsed onto the nearest chair and sank her head in her hands, the picture of dejection and defeat. Amanda was certain Richard would do no such thing, but her mother didn't know him as well as she did.

'He's concerned about your losses at cards. If you refrain from playing for a week or two, I'm sure it will all blow over and you'll be on good terms again.'

Her mother jerked upright, her expression hard, her eyes like slate. A shiver of apprehension slithered down Amanda's spine. She was facing a woman she didn't recognise, and one she didn't like.

'Your dear departed father allowed

me to spend my allowance as I pleased. If I overspent, he happily picked up my debts. This man is not fit to replace your father. I'll never like him, and I intend to ensure that no one else does either.'

Amanda gripped the back of the chair, shocked to the core by this vitriolic outpouring. 'Mama, I suggest that you think about your actions before you do anything you regret. Richard could cut off your allowance with a snap of his fingers, send you away . . .'

'I might have known you would be on his side. You were always your father's favourite, and never had time for me when he was alive. You have poisoned your sisters against me . . .'

\* \* \*

'Silence. You will not address Amanda like that. Your unpleasantness was heard by everyone in the house. You should be ashamed of yourself to speak in that way about someone who puts everyone ahead of her own interests, and has never done anything but behave as a dutiful and loving daughter to you.'

Richard had not been exaggerating about the dowager's outburst carrying throughout the house. He'd heard her from the library and come at once to put a stop to it. The woman wasn't rational. There was only one explanation, and that was that her need to gamble was so deep-seated that being denied this had turned her mind.

He had moved to stand protectively behind Amanda, and she glanced up at him, her eyes brimming.

He touched her elbow gently, and she understood his gesture as one of support. He stood, alert, waiting to fend off the next barrage of unpleasantness. The look he got was venom-filled.

'This is my domain, sir, and you are intruding. Kindly remove yourself from my presence at once.'

'You forget yourself, madam, you are here at my sufferance. As your daughter so rightly pointed out, I could send you north if I so wished, and there would be nothing you could do about it.'

'Then I shall move elsewhere. I have friends here, which you do not. I shall avail myself of their hospitality.' Her lips were thin, her eyes dark with rage. 'You will regret this, sir, I give you my word on that.'

She swept past them, head held high, and he knew he'd made a dangerous enemy — one that could not only harm him but, more importantly, the woman he loved and the girls he'd come to regard as his dear sisters.

He kicked the door shut as he had no wish to be heard by any lurking servant. Amanda was trembling. He didn't hesitate, but gathered her into his arms, and she wept against his shoulder whilst he offered what comfort he could in an impossible situation.

'Sweetheart, dry your eyes; we must talk. I mishandled this dreadfully, and fear I've permanently alienated the duchess.'

She sniffed and dried her eyes in the handkerchief he'd given her. 'This is the worst I've ever seen her. She has a dreadful temper, but has never unleashed it on me before. It's as though she's always hated me, and has only been pretending these past years to be a loving parent.'

He led her to the sofa and sat down beside her, still holding her hand in his. 'The only way I can explain this is by telling you about something that happened in Portugal last year. A fellow officer, one I'd considered a good friend, was always first at the card table, but I'd no inkling that he was addicted to the pastime.

'Our commanding officer heard that he'd been winning, fleecing younger officers, and stepped in, ordering him to stop playing forthwith.'

'What did he do?'

'Exactly what just happened, only with far worse consequences for him. He struck the colonel in his rage, and was court-martialled and dismissed from the service — if he'd been from the ranks, he'd have been flogged or worse.'

Her smile was watery but at least she was no longer crying. 'Good heavens! What could be worse than a flogging?'

'A common soldier might well have been hanged.'

'Mama has always played for high stakes, but Papa didn't seem to be at all put out by this. She was right to say he paid her gambling debts without question, and never threatened to send her to live in Northumbria.'

'Then all I can say is that I wish he had taken a firmer stand, then we wouldn't be in this situation now. I'm in an invidious position. It would be easier if I was her son, and not a man she considers an interloper.'

'She does have friends amongst the most important families, and could make things horrible for all of us.'

'I was told that being a duke meant I could do as I pleased and everyone would accept it. Are you telling me this isn't the case?'

'It is, of course. However, she's the Dowager Duchess of Denchester, is the daughter of an earl . . .'

There was no need for her to finish her sentence: the implications were quite clear. The duchess would have more influence over society's opinion than he would.

'What do you suggest I do about it?' he mused. 'My instinct is to retreat to the country and let them gossip how they wish about us. I also intend to cut off her allowance. This will stop her playing. She cannot remain with friends indefinitely, and will come home to us so we can repair the damage.'

'Run away? Fiddlesticks to that. We must all go somewhere we shall be seen tonight, and you must demonstrate your credentials by being charming and aristocratic.'

He raised an eyebrow, and she laughed. 'The first I can do, but I fear I know little about the second.'

'Just remember your military background, and then look down your nose at everybody — that will do perfectly. I must tell Sarah what happened, and then look through the invitations to see if there's somewhere suitable for tonight. Miss Westley must come, and also Mr O'Riley.'

★　★　★

He made himself scarce in the library until the dowager had made her noisy departure — with so many boxes and trunks that it took two carriages to convey them wherever she was moving to.

O'Riley came to see him during the afternoon. 'Your grace, her grace has gone to stay with the Earl of Nantwich. From what I gleaned from talking to their staff, she's not a welcome guest. I think that her plan to destroy your good name will come to naught.'

'I don't like to think of her unhappy, despite her behaviour. I sincerely hope

252

we can mend the rift before it becomes permanent. Gambling is an addiction as dangerous as drinking and smoking opium. I've no notion how to move forward from here.' He rubbed his eyes, and wished he was safely back on the Peninsula, where he knew what he was doing and could solve any problem and fight any battle in full command of the situation.

* * *

There was a tentative knock on the door an hour or so later, and Amanda came in waving an invitation card. 'I've sent word to Lady Eastham that we'll be attending her rout. Hers is the furthest house from us on this side, but still close enough to walk unless the weather is inclement.'

The words were accompanied by the rattle of rain on the windowpanes. 'It will be a tight squeeze in one carriage, but I'm damned if I'll have two used for such a short journey.'

253

'I know things are difficult, but could you please refrain from using such bad language all the time? My nerves are in shreds already without your immoderate speech.'

'I apologise. I seem to be doing a lot of that lately. Civilian life is so much more complicated than the military one.'

'I suppose being in command of your soldiers and trying to keep them alive whilst killing your enemies might be considered a calm and ordered existence to you — but to me it would be a nightmare.'

'I should think so. War's not a suitable place for a gently born lady such as yourself.'

'I thought that wives of officers often travelled with them.'

'There have been one or two, but it's not something I approve of. A soldier needs to have all his attention on the matter in hand, and not be worrying about his beloved.'

She delved into her pocket and

waved his list at him.

'I also came to discuss this. This exactly describes me — I'm not sure I appreciate your humour.'

Something she didn't recognise flickered in his eyes, but then he smiled and she thought herself mistaken. 'I suppose I must apologise yet again. It was by way of a hint to you that I'm perfectly capable of finding my own wife.'

'And I, if I wished to, could find myself a comfortable husband.' She tilted her head and pouted in a parody of a debutante. 'You might not be aware of it, your grace, but I'm the daughter of a duke, an heiress, and I'm not quite bracket-faced.'

His snort of laughter made her giggle too. 'I've told you before, you're a baggage. Fishing for compliments? You'll find none from me. You know exactly what I think of you, and I don't intend to make your head swell even bigger.'

'Then we shall call it quits. I shan't parade a string of hopeful young ladies in front of you, and you will not introduce me to eligible bachelors.'

'Then we shall return to our original plan, the one you will recall that we discussed. We'll dance once with each other, and then stand as guards behind Sarah's chair.'

'You're forgetting that you must dance with my sister before me. She's the one making her debut, and you must be seen to approve of her.'

'I do more than that: I'm inordinately fond of you all. I heard what happened with Beth this afternoon. I think it best if she doesn't go out of the square unless either O'Riley or myself are present.'

'Miss Bennett will be here in a few days looking for Mama — what shall we tell her?'

'That she and I had a difference of opinion, and she's gone off in high dudgeon but is expected back when she's recovered her temper.'

'Should we send her to join my mother, or keep her here in the hope that everything returns to normal?'

'I'll leave you to decide that particular question. What time do we leave for this event?'

'I will arrange for trays to be sent to our apartments. Supper will be served at the venue, but not until ten or eleven o'clock.'

★　★　★

Amanda picked at her tray; her appetite had deserted her after the upset earlier. She scarcely noticed what gown her abigail had selected for her. She dreaded the thought that her mother would be at the same event and already causing problems for them all. Papa had allowed the gambling to become an addiction, and if he'd stepped in, they wouldn't be in this predicament now.

She found it strange that her parents had been living separate lives for as long as she could remember, but yet her father had indulged her mother in a way that indicated he still had feelings for her.

She had no cousins, no aunts or uncles, no grandparents to make enquiries from, so would have to remain in ignorance of what had been the true state of affairs.

Sarah drifted in, lovely in a silver gown with a pale blue underskirt. 'I wish we didn't have to go, Amanda. In fact, I've changed my mind about being in Town. Do you think you could persuade Richard to cancel my ball and take us home?'

'He would take no persuading, my love, he's already suggested it himself. I told him a soldier never retreats, and reluctantly he agreed to remain here until we've persuaded our mother to return to us.'

'Then I must enjoy it for his sake. That's a very daring colour, sister. I don't recall you ordering anything in emerald green.'

She looked down at her ensemble in surprise. 'I'd quite forgotten I'd got this one. It is a little outrageous for someone my age. Mama would have a conniption fit if she saw us tonight. You in silver and blue, and me in startling green.'

Richard spoke from the door where he was leaning nonchalantly against the frame, resplendent in his evening black. 'I'll be the envy of every gentleman tonight escorting you two beautiful young ladies. By the by, Miss Westley and O'Riley have decided to walk across the square to the venue, which means we won't be squashed in the carriage.'

'They should have come with us. I don't like the idea of them walking in the wet. Miss Westley's shoes and gown will be quite ruined by the rain.'

'It stopped raining an hour ago. If you two are ready, shall we depart? I don't like to keep the horses waiting even when the weather's clement.'

He handed both of them into the carriage and then jumped in himself, making it rock alarmingly. They scarcely had time to settle before they were joining the queue of vehicles waiting to deliver the occupants at the front door.

Sarah looked out of the carriage window. 'There are flambeaux and a red carpet leading to the door. Shall I have such extravagances at my ball, Richard?'

'If that's what you want, then it will be arranged. Let's get this over with — the sooner we can go home again, the better.'

She laughed at his less-than-enthusiastic comment. 'Come now, sir, think of this as a military campaign. We're here for the sole purpose of showing you at your best — and you are to contradict, by your charm and wit, any unpleasantness that might have already been spoken about you.'

# 14

Richard hadn't been exaggerating when he'd said he'd be the envy of everyone present. They were a handsome party, the five of them, as they made their entrance to this prestigious event.

Heads turned. The gentlemen stared, not only at Amanda and Sarah, who looked quite beautiful, but also at Miss Westley. She was on the arm of Patrick and, although older than the majority of young ladies present, she was by no means eclipsed by them. If Richard hadn't already fallen in love with Amanda, he might well have taken an interest in her companion.

Lord and Lady Whoever seemed inordinately pleased that they'd come, despite their late acceptance of the invitation. There were not that many dukes in the country, so he supposed even one not born to the job was better than none at all.

He nodded, smiled and bowed when appropriate, and was heartily sick of the whole business by the time they were able to move towards the ballroom.

This space had been decked out in all manner of frills, furbelows and flowers for the evening. It looked quite ridiculous, in his opinion. The quartet at the far end of the room was tuning up, and sounded like four cats in a bag.

Then he remembered that all he needed to do was look down his nose and walk like a soldier. His lips curved and he couldn't quite hide his amusement.

Amanda had her hand through his left arm, walking proudly beside him, and tonight her limp was imperceptible. Sarah was on his other side, equally beautiful and equally proud.

'I'm glad you're no longer scowling, Richard; you look less formidable when you smile,' she told him.

'Am I looking down my nose sufficiently to impress the other guests with my importance?'

Sarah giggled and hid her face behind her fan.

Amanda smiled. 'I was jesting when I said that, as you very well know. Mr O'Riley has found us an excellent place where we can keep an eye on things without being trampled on by those wishing to dance.'

Sarah was the only one amongst them who seemed excited to be there. Patrick looked as uncomfortable as he did, and neither Amanda nor Miss Westley appeared enthusiastic about prancing around the ballroom.

'Is this considered to be a ball or just an informal dance?'

'To be honest, I'm not sure what this is,' she replied. 'I'm not aware that it's to launch a hopeful daughter on the marriage mart, and I can't recall exactly what was written on the invitation, can you?'

The ladies had now settled like colourful birds upon the frail gilt chairs set out around the edges of the room. If he or Patrick attempted to sit on one it would collapse beneath them, no doubt causing much hilarity to those watching and embarrassment to themselves. Tonight they must both remain on their feet.

Miss Westley overheard, and with a polite smile entered the conversation. 'They have twin sons of marriageable age, and this event is in honour of them reaching their majority.' She gestured with her head towards two identical, dark-haired spindly youths in violently striped waistcoats which clashed horribly with their black evening dress.

Sarah spoke from behind her open fan. 'I do hope I don't have to dance with either of them. I've decided that when and if I do take a husband, it will be to a much older gentleman like yourself, Richard, not an unformed boy like those two.'

He choked back his laughter at being referred to as an older gentleman. 'A wise decision, sweetheart, as I'd not let either of those jackanapes anywhere near you.'

'It's a sad crush in here already, and I fear it will get worse once the dancing starts. Why on earth have they not opened the doors and windows at the far end to let some fresh air in here?'

'Patrick and I can do that for you, Amanda . . . '

Her eyes widened as if he'd said something unpardonable. 'No, you cannot do such a thing. Servants open windows, not dukes.' Her smile made him want to take her in his arms. 'And anyway, it's not our business to interfere with the running of the household. It would be the height of bad manners to demand that windows are opened the moment we arrived.'

The musicians, if one could call them that, struck up a lively air; and the two young men, for whom this event had been put on, led out a pair of matching insipid young ladies.

'Do I dance with you first, Amanda, or your sister?'

'I have precedence as I'm the eldest, so I suppose it must be me.'

'I'll remain with Lady Sarah, my lady, so you may join a set with a clear conscience.'

He was about to hold out his hand and lead her forward when the hostess sailed towards them with half a dozen eager young, and not so young, gentlemen behind her.

Each of these hopeful suitors was introduced to Amanda and Sarah, and he didn't like the look of any of them. One thing he did know, as she had explained it to him, was that if he gave his permission for his charges to dance then they must accept the first gentleman that asked them. If they refused to dance with anyone suitable, then they could not dance for the remainder of the evening. The ridiculous rule meant Sarah had the unenviable task of dancing with one of those that had just been introduced.

She looked to him for guidance and he selected the least objectionable of the six. 'You have my permission to dance with Lord Sydney, Lady Sarah.'

She held out a hand to this gentleman and he took it eagerly. The disappointed went in search of other partners, but would no doubt return.

\* \* \*

So far Amanda hadn't detected any sideways glances or disapproving looks from those assembled. Did this mean that their mother had changed her mind, or that any malicious gossip had yet to spread?

'It's so long since I've danced in public that I fear I might trip over my feet and will tread on your toes, Richard.'

'As long as I don't step on yours, we've nothing to worry about.'

The other couples eager to join a set moved aside to allow them to take the third place in the first set, behind the twins.

'I wonder which of them will inherit

the title and estates?' Amanda mused. 'It must be a bone of contention to find that someone identical to yourself, but born a few minutes earlier, gets everything and you are left with nothing.'

'Personally, I think one should be able to leave one's money and title to the most deserving in the family, rather than the eldest.'

'I seem to recall from my history lessons when I was a schoolgirl that hundreds of years ago brothers murdered each other in order to inherit.'

'That's a different thing entirely. However, in other cultures the reigning king, sultan or whatever, did have the choice — no doubt this too led to assassinations.'

Despite his dislike of dancing, being partnered by her made it an enjoyable experience. It was a simple country dance and neither of them had missed a step. When the final chords died away, he bowed, she curtsied, and he then turned to escort her to the safety of their companions.

The chairs were empty but a footman stood guard over them. He grinned and sloped off when they arrived. Richard looked around and saw Patrick returning with Miss Westley, both looking remarkably pleased with themselves.

Amanda was already seated and he stood behind her so he could speak without being overheard. 'I didn't know he could dance — not something a sergeant major is required to do, unlike an officer. I wonder where he learned the steps?'

'Miss Westley taught him. I know this, as I was asked to play for them. As he was going to be escorting us, he wanted to be proficient and not draw attention to himself by being unable to take a turn on the dance floor.'

Sarah had scarcely arrived at their side before she was off again with another of those she'd been introduced to earlier.

'Do I have to dance with anyone else?'

'You must dance with Miss Westley and I shall dance with Mr O'Riley. Then you must dance with Sarah, but I don't see why you have to mingle any more than that.'

'I intend to dance with you a second time — I believe that's allowed?'

'As I'm already considered fast because I'm wearing emerald green instead of a pastel shade, I hardly think it matters how many times we dance.'

'My dear Lady Amanda, I beg you, do not break the rules on your first appearance. I'm sure you don't wish to add fuel to the fire that her grace might be starting.'

'Thank you for reminding me. I'll not upset the tabbies further. On that subject, I've not noticed other guests viewing us with disfavour — have you?'

'No, not at all. In fact, they could not have been more conciliatory and friendly.' Miss Westley smiled shyly at Richard. 'For the first time in my life, I've been treated as if I deserved to be in this company. I do believe that being a member of your party, your grace, has raised my status somewhat.'

Mr O'Riley nodded vigorously. 'This is the first grand event I've attended, and I must say that it's not as unpleasant as I'd expected it to be.'

Amanda laughed. 'Good heavens, sir, one must not say such things in company. One might think them, but not express them out loud.'

Richard's fingers tightened on the back of her chair. What had alarmed him? She looked over her shoulder and saw a handsome gentleman with dark hair and even darker eyes approaching them. He took one look at her escort's forbidding features and turned away as if going somewhere else entirely.

'That unfortunate gentleman was coming to ask me to dance with him. Now you have denied me that pleasure, your grace. I thought the object of this exercise was to demonstrate your good nature, good breeding and good gracious . . .'

He stared at her as if she was

speaking in tongues, and then followed the direction of her anguished glance. Mama was approaching like a burgundy ship in full sail, and from her expression it wasn't a friendly visit.

They were all standing when she arrived. As others were watching, Amanda curtsied politely, as did her sister and Miss Westley. Richard and Mr O'Riley bowed. Mama merely nodded.

'Good evening, your grace, would you care to join us?' Richard said smoothly.

Mama raked him from head to toe and found him wanting. Amanda braced herself for some sort of tirade that would be the main topic of conversation at every breakfast table the following morning.

'I came to tell you, sir, that I am leaving. I do so because I have no wish to be in the same establishment as yourself.'

He nodded. 'How kind of you to walk the length of the ballroom in order to inform me. I shall have a list of our future engagements sent to your present domicile so that in future you may avoid another meeting.'

There was little point in trying to reason with this woman who was like a stranger to them. Amanda dipped again, as did the other two, and then her mother stalked off with a rustle of silk and bombazine.

There was a collective sigh of relief that the confrontation had been no worse than it was.

'Thank goodness Mama didn't raise her voice. I think what happened might well have gone unnoticed,' Sarah said.

'I hate to disabuse you, my dear, but everyone within earshot heard every word. It will be common knowledge now that the Dowager Duchess of Denchester is at odds with her family.'

★ ★ ★

'Is there anything we can do to remedy the situation, Richard? Perhaps things would improve if you reinstated her allowance.'

'That isn't going to happen. Your mother's becoming a hardened gambler, and I must take a stand now if matters are not going to be out of hand in the future.'

'Quickly, dance with Sarah before the twin with the purple-and-gold waistcoat arrives to ask her to stand up with him.'

'Then it will fall to you to dance with him instead. If that's your wish, then I'll follow your command.'

Sarah needed no second bidding and was at his side in an instant. As they walked to join another set, she whispered to him, 'I'll dance with one other gentleman as well as Mr O'Riley, you still have to dance with Miss Westley, then we can go home, can't we? Please tell me we don't have to stay until supper?'

'I fear that we do. We must brazen it out as if nothing untoward has taken place, as if the public falling out with your mother is a commonplace occurrence and nothing that bothers us.'

By the time he and Patrick had danced with all three of the ladies in his party, the guests were beginning to drift into the supper room. Miss Westley had gone ahead and reserved a table for them.

The food might have been delicious but he scarcely noticed. He was as eager as the others to leave. They made their farewells to their host and hostess, nodded and smiled to any who looked their way, and finally escaped from the over-perfumed atmosphere and heat of the crowded ballroom.

Two footmen from his house were waiting to escort them across the square with flaming torches. The girls rushed off together, leaving him and Patrick to walk behind.

'That was an experience I'd prefer not to repeat, your grace. I can't fathom why some folk want to spend every night at an event like that.'

'Unfortunately, my friend, we're

committed to three similar occasions each week that we're here. Just be thankful we don't have to accompany our ladies on morning calls, or be in the drawing room to receive visitors when it's their turn.'

'For all her bravado, as far as I could discover, her grace hasn't spread any unpleasantness about you.'

'I think that her dramatic departure was meant to indicate her disapproval. I intend to leave it for a few days and then offer an olive branch.'

He received a letter by express early the following morning that put the irritating business of her grace out of his mind. He was urgently needed at Denchester Hall, and had to return there at once.

He quickly penned a note to Amanda, explaining where he'd gone and that he'd return as soon as he could. Then he sent for his man.

'You must stand escort in my stead, Patrick, I'll be back by the end of the week, hopefully. I'm going to travel post

— exorbitantly expensive, but can't be helped.'

'You can be assured, your grace, that I'll take the best care of your charges in your absence. Miss Westley suggested that we take a drive in the park later this morning.'

'I think that Lady Amanda will prefer to ride. You will accompany her on my gelding — Lady Elizabeth and Lady Sarah will be safe with Miss Westley in the carriage as long as you remain alongside.'

★ ★ ★

Richard dealt with the problems that had occurred when the builders had begun to demolish the main structure. The reclamation of the materials to use in the new building was proving time-consuming and difficult. After discussions with the architects, he decided it would be simpler in the long run to start afresh.

'Just save what you can, but getting

on with the work is paramount. I want my new home ready for occupation by the end of next year at the latest.'

His factor, knowing he would be there, arrived with half a dozen other matters relating to the estates. One was of great interest to him.

'The tenant for Radley Manor has left and the house is now unoccupied, your grace.'

'Take me there — it's somewhere I've not yet visited. As Denchester won't be ready for occupation for a considerable time, I need to find somewhere else to live meanwhile.' What he meant, but obviously wasn't going to say, was that he wanted an estate where he could start his married life with Amanda.

Radley was perfect. Larger than the Dower House, and of more recent construction, so needed little doing to it to make it ready for his new bride. There was ample room for his future sisters-in-law and their retainers, and a separate annexe which would be ideal for Patrick. He intended that his mother-in-law remain in the Dower House where she belonged.

He was relishing the peace and quiet of the countryside, but knew he must return to his duties in Town. He hadn't enjoyed travelling at breakneck speed in a post-chaise and was determined to ride his second gelding back to London. It would take a day longer, but would be worth it, as then Patrick would also have a decent mount to ride when he went out.

He was woken by a thunderous knocking on his bedchamber door. He was awake and out of bed instantly; he snatched up his bedrobe and flung open the door. The butler, more or less dressed, handed him a letter on a silver salver that had arrived by express.

*Richard,*
   *You must return at once. The most dreadful thing has happened and Beth now finds herself compromised. The young gentleman concerned, the oldest son of Lord*

279

*Eastham, one of the twins we met the other night, mistook her for Sarah.*

*I cannot bear to write any more. I beg you, come immediately.*

*Amanda*

# 15

During the first two days of Richard's absence Amanda was relieved that nothing alarming took place. They attended a musical evening — which was quite excruciating — and both made and received morning calls. There had been no word from their mama, and the house seemed empty with both her and Richard gone. The only drawback to these proceedings was the fact that both of Lord Eastham's twins were now pursuing Sarah. Her sister was no more than polite to either of them, but they were proving most insistent. She would be relieved when Richard returned and put a stop to their pretensions.

Beth was enjoying the few excursions she was allowed to take, and no one who didn't know the circumstances would have thought her anything but a lovely young lady, not yet out, enjoying the events of the Season that she was allowed to attend.

On the third day Miss Westley approached with a suggestion. 'There's to be a firework display at Vauxhall Gardens, Lady Amanda, this evening. I was wondering if we could attend as long as Mr O'Riley and two footmen came with us? Lady Elizabeth is desperate to go, and so I agreed to ask you.'

'The weather's perfect for an outdoor excursion. I see no reason why not. I believe that we need to book a booth where we can have supper and watch in privacy. As long as we don't wander about with the crowds, then I'm sure that his grace wouldn't object to us going.'

'Do you wish me to make the arrangements, my lady?'

'Yes, that would be splendid. Miss Bennett is due to arrive at any moment, and I've the difficult task of explaining the present circumstances and discovering if she still wishes to be in her grace's employ.'

Her mother's companion was suitably shocked by the revelation of what had taken place. 'Forgive me, my lady, but as long as I can have a good reference, I'd much prefer to terminate my employment. Whilst I was away I was fortunate to be offered another post, that of companion to a delightful old lady I've known for years. Of course, if things were as they should be, I wouldn't even consider accepting it.'

'I'll write your reference now, Miss Bennett, and wish you every happiness in your new position.'

The meeting ended with both satisfied with the outcome. Amanda had also paid the back wages owed, and included an extra guinea to pay for travel. She was eagerly anticipating the visit to Vauxhall and both her sisters were overjoyed to be going.

In the carriage she spoke sternly to them both — although Sarah knew very well the homily was aimed at Beth, not herself.

'You will walk beside me at all times.

You will not speak to anyone unless I give you leave. We shall remain together in our booth and only leave the safety of this place when we're ready to return. Is that quite clear?'

'I promise, Amanda, I promise I'll be a good girl and stay with Miss Westley. Will there be dancing? Can I join in?'

'Beth, what did I just tell you? There will be no dancing for any of us even if there is any. We remain inside the booth and don't interact or converse with anyone else.'

She was beginning to have doubts about the safety of this outing, but it was too late to repine. She glanced across at Miss Westley. 'Lady Elizabeth will remain with me. We shall all have an excellent time and enjoy the firework display.'

Mr O'Riley was sitting next to Amanda and he nodded his agreement. 'His grace asked me to act in his stead on any outings, and I intend to do so. I give you my word nothing alarming will take place tonight.'

'Fireworks are alarming, Mr O'Riley, they are ever so noisy and bright and sometimes I have to cover my ears and close my eyes.'

'That's very true, Lady Elizabeth, but we shall all be safe in our own private room.'

They arrived at the venue after an uneventful journey across the river and Amanda began to relax and enjoy herself. This was a place she'd never attended and she was enjoying it as much as the others.

Mr O'Riley strode ahead, clearing the way for them, and the two footmen carrying the picnic baskets walked directly behind them, preventing any unwanted gentlemen from accosting the party.

Miss Westley had procured a perfect spot. They were all enchanted by the little chamber set aside for them. 'Excellent, we'll be able to see everything perfectly from here. Now, Beth, where do you want to sit?'

There were jugglers, stilt-walkers and

fire-eaters to entertain them whilst they waited for the main event. The picnic supper was set out on the tables and every morsel was eaten. The crowds had doubled as hundreds of visitors arrived to see the display. Miss Westley had sole charge of Beth, who had been perfectly behaved.

Amanda looked up. 'Beth, it's about to start. Do you wish to come to the front where you can see even more clearly?'

'Miss Westley has taken her to the ladies' retiring rooms. Mr O'Riley has accompanied them,' Sarah answered.

Instantly, she was on her feet. 'This is most upsetting. I should have been consulted first. I don't like the idea of Beth being out in this crowd as she could be separated from her escorts.' She spoke to the two footmen who were busy repacking the picnic baskets. 'Both of you, go out at once and make sure that Lady Elizabeth is kept safe.'

They vanished. Everyone employed by the family understood the situation.

She scanned the crowd in the hope of seeing Mr O'Riley. He was taller than most gentlemen and should be easy to spot.

'Where exactly are these retiring rooms?'

'You cannot see them from the front, Amanda, but if you recall, we passed the building just before we reached this booth. It's only a few minutes from here. I'm sure our sister can manage to get there and back without anything unpleasant occurring.' Sarah gestured at the milling crowds. 'Everyone's here to watch the fireworks and has no interest in anything else.'

'I pray that you're right. How long have they been gone?'

'No more than ten minutes. Do you wish to go in search of them?'

'We cannot do so without a male escort. We must remain here and pray they all return safely in a few minutes.'

The minutes stretched to twenty, and neither the footmen nor Miss Westley, Beth or Mr O'Riley, had returned. The fireworks display had begun, and it was impossible to hold a conversation above the noise of the explosions and the roars of approval coming from the crowd.

'I can't stay here a moment longer. I must go out and look for them.'

'No, Amanda, that will just make things worse. There are gentlemen the worse for drink out there, and no doubt common men, thieves and pickpockets as well, just looking for an unwary female on her own.'

Her sister was right to warn her, but she couldn't just wait when she knew that something dreadful must have happened.

She went to the door in the rear of the booth and opened it, but remained inside where she was safe. Sarah joined her and together they searched the crush, hoping to see the distinctive livery of their footmen, or one of the other three.

Amanda was beside herself when half an hour had passed and there was still no sign of any of them. Then she saw Mr O'Riley — walking fast, his arm around Beth, and Miss Westley holding her hand.

They saw her in the doorway and pointed to the exit. The two footmen arrived at a run. 'You go ahead, my lady, we'll bring the baskets. We'll be right behind you.'

A servant shouldn't give instructions to their employers, but in this case it was acceptable. Both Amanda and Sarah already had their evening cloaks around their shoulders, and they rushed across and fell in behind the other three.

It was impossible to see Beth's face, as her head was lowered and her bonnet brim too deep. The fact that she wasn't crying, protesting or making a sound filled Amanda with a sick dread. There was only one thing that would make her sister silent. Beth had been so frightened by something that she was unable to function normally. The last time this had happened was when her pony had bolted with her, and she hadn't ridden a horse since then.

★ ★ ★

Richard arrived in London thirty-six hours after receiving the letter. He was travel-worn and weary, and his resemblance to a brigand was remarkable. When he dismounted in the stable yard the head groom was speechless.

'I've ridden him hard and he'll need to be walked until he's cool. No water until then.'

He strode towards the house and despite his precipitous arrival he was already expected. The side door was flung open and Amanda burst through and threw herself into his arms.

'Thank God you're here, I've been at my wits' end to know what to do. The only member of the household unconcerned by this catastrophe is the perpetrator — Beth remains oblivious and continues on as if nothing had happened at all.'

'The library, my love — we must continue this conversation in private.'

He didn't apologise for his dishevelled state, and his beloved appeared not to notice he wasn't fit to be in her company as he was. 'I should change . . . ' he added belatedly.

'No, come as you are. Refreshments will be here at any moment. I've not been able to eat a morsel since we went to the Vauxhall Gardens.'

They'd scarcely entered the chamber when two footmen followed them with laden trays, small beer and two jugs of coffee. These were placed on the central table and then the servants vanished.

He removed his gloves and topcoat and tossed them onto a nearby chair. At least his hands were relatively clean, even if the rest of his person was malodorous.

He was shocked at her appearance. Her eyes were dark, her face etched with worry. 'Sit down, Amanda, and we shall eat before we talk. I'm exhausted and need refreshment urgently.'

She didn't protest, but merely settled into the nearest chair without a murmur. He didn't make the mistake of piling her plate, just put a few tasty morsels on one and then poured her a cup of coffee.

He snatched up a pasty and ate that where he stood. This was closely followed by a second, and then a third. He then downed a pint of small beer and was ready to hear the details of this disaster.

'I've never seen anyone devour so much so quickly, Richard. Did you not eat on your journey?'

This time he put a selection on a plate and picked up the necessary cutlery and napkin before joining her. 'I can't remember, but I suppose I must have grabbed a sandwich or two. My concern was for my mount, as without him staying on his feet I'd not have got here so speedily.'

Her plate was also empty, and he refilled it and her cup before taking his place beside her.

'Now we're more or less replete, tell me what happened. If Beth is well, then obviously she wasn't molested, which was what I feared.'

'No, thank the Lord. Just before the fireworks display, she wished to visit the retiring room, and Mr O'Riley and Miss Westley accompanied her. There were so many people milling about that they became separated, despite Miss Westley having had hold of her hand.

'Lord Eastham's son mistook her for Sarah, and invited her to take a promenade around a secluded garden. Beth thought it a lark that he supposed her to be our sister, and agreed to go with him. He put his arm around her, and they were seen embracing — and recognised — by several of our acquaintances.' She was unable to continue, and he wanted to comfort her, but that would be taking advantage of her distress.

'Go on, tell me the rest. It doesn't matter how bad it is, I can put matters right.'

'Beth became bored with the rendez-vous and, on seeing Miss Westley and Mr O'Riley approaching, detached herself and ran to them.'

'What happened next?'

'My sister was severely taken to task by Miss Westley, and was more upset by that than by the embrace. When I saw them, I imagined the worst. It wasn't until Beth had been sent to bed in disgrace that I discovered exactly what had transpired.'

'I think I can guess what you're going to tell me — what the real disaster is. That snivelling youth insists that Sarah marries him, and you have either to reveal that Beth is a simpleton or have your other sister's good name ruined.'

'Sarah refused to speak to him when he called, which has just made him more determined. Lady Eastham arrived yesterday, demanding that she speak to you, and insisting that the betrothal must be announced immediately.'

'I'll see Eastham. By the time I've finished with him and his son, they'll rue their interference in our lives. You do understand, don't you, sweetheart, that the only way out of this is to tell them the truth about Beth? As she doesn't mix in society, I can't see that will cause her any distress.'

'Our parents always said they'd not tarnish Beth with such a label. But you're right — it's the only solution to this problem.' She reached out and took his hand. 'Promise me, Richard, that you don't intend to do anything violent.'

He raised her hand to his lips and kissed her knuckles, and then released her. 'I give you my word. I'd dearly love to horsewhip that bastard, but will refrain.'

He was about to apologise for his intemperate language when she laughed. 'I suppose I must become used to your swearing, as it doesn't seem that any amount of complaint on my part makes the slightest bit of difference.'

'I'm only a rough soldier at heart, my

love, and it might well take you years to smooth me into shape.'

Her cheeks flushed becomingly, and in that moment, he knew she'd changed her mind about him being a suitable husband. Before she could move, he dropped to one knee.

'Darling girl, I love you to distraction. I don't give a damn about the rules. Will you do me the inestimable honour of becoming my wife?'

For a moment she didn't answer, and he held his breath, thinking for a second that he'd misunderstood the situation.

'Please stand up, Richard, and stop making a cake of yourself. I discovered that I too am in love with you. I should be delighted to accept your kind offer.'

Instead of standing, he reached up and tumbled her onto his lap. She returned his kisses with enthusiasm, and it took all his iron control to regain his feet with her still in his arms and put her back on the chair.

★ ★ ★

Amanda glowed from the tips of her toes to the crown of her head and was so happy she thought she might burst. Then reality stuck and she regained command of her senses.

'This must remain between us, my love, until the matter with the Easthams has been settled and my mother has returned to the bosom of her family. I know you don't have to ask her permission to marry me, but I can't make our betrothal public until I have her blessing.'

'I don't care how long we have to wait — no, that's nonsense. I want to marry you as soon as it can be arranged. June is supposed to be the perfect month for a wedding.'

'That would be wonderful, but until things are resolved and the family restored, things must remain as they are between us. I don't even want to tell Sarah.'

'As you wish. I'm going to bathe and

change my raiment, and then will visit Eastham. Have you detected any coolness towards the family in the past few days?'

'I cancelled all our engagements on the pretext that we have suffered from a sudden and highly contagious ailment picked up at the Vauxhall Gardens. Therefore, I've no idea if any gossip about the incident the other night or anything else has changed society's opinion of us.'

'Sensible girl. We'll discover how things are on our next excursion. Go and tell your sister and Miss Westley. What is planned for tonight, if anything?'

'It's the first of the major balls. The Earl of Colchester is launching his daughter, and it's likely to be the event of the Season.' She hesitated, not sure if she should mention that it was a masquerade. His eyes narrowed, and he raised an eyebrow. 'We have to go in costume and with masks.'

Instead of being cross, he smiled his toe-curling smile. 'And what exactly have you planned for me?'

'You can go as a soldier — I thought you probably had your best regimentals in one of the trunks that arrived last week from somewhere on the continent.'

'Not a Roman centurion? Not a Greek god? You disappoint me, darling — I would have enjoyed watching you try to persuade me to wear something ridiculous.'

'It would have been a waste of my breath, so I didn't bother.' She waited until he was through the door before calling after him, 'I'm going as Lady Godiva!'

She could hear him laughing as he strode away, and wanted to turn cartwheels across the library, but thought she might cast up her accounts if she did so, having just eaten so much.

* * *

Both Sarah and Miss Westley agreed with the decision to tell the world about

299

Beth's disability.

'What did Richard say about attending the masquerade ball tonight?'

'He was remarkably sanguine about the whole thing. I even said that I was going as Lady Godiva, and he just laughed.'

'Good gracious, my lady, that was a risque thing to suggest,' Miss Westley exclaimed.

'I didn't tell him we were going as three Greek goddesses and will be dressed in diaphanous gowns. Is Mr O'Riley coming as a soldier?'

'No. I suggested it, but he was adamant he would come as Zeus to complement our costumes.'

'Then Richard will look out of place — I think I might try and change his mind and get him to appear as King Neptune.'

Mr O'Riley, who had just joined them, grinned. 'I wish you good luck with that, my lady. I'd stake my right arm on him refusing.'

'If you will excuse me, I must speak

to Nancy, my head seamstress, and get her and her girls busy making a costume fit for a king — even if it is of the sea.' She frowned. 'I think perhaps that Hades, King of the Underworld, might be more appropriate. I'll give the matter further thought.'

# 16

Richard dressed to impress, and even carried his beaver and cane under one arm and wore gloves. He looked every inch an aristocrat, although his blood was so diluted he could scarcely think of himself as such. Then it occurred to him that if his great-great-grandfather had been the older brother, he would have been born and bred a duke.

He crossed the central park and walked up to the front door of Eastham's establishment. Only then did it occur to him he should have brought a footman to knock in his stead. He banged so hard he was certain no one could ignore him.

The door opened, and a supercilious butler was about to give him his comeuppance, but then wisely reconsidered.

'Duke of Denchester. Take me to Lord Eastham.' The man hesitated. 'Take me now,' Richard snarled, and the man quailed beneath his contempt. 'At once, your grace. If you would care to follow me, I believe that his lordship is in his study.'

Richard stalked behind him and waited until the trembling butler knocked. 'My lord, his grace the Duke of Denchester is here to see you.'

He didn't give Eastham the chance to respond, but stepped around the butler and marched straight in. He stood ramrod-straight and nodded at Eastham, who'd been lounging on the sofa blowing a cloud and had barely had time to spring to his feet.

'Your grace, this is an unexpected pleasure. I thought you in the country.'

'Obviously not. I am most displeased with your behaviour and that of your objectionable son. If I was still an officer I would have him flogged for his mistreatment of Lady Elizabeth.'

'Lady Elizabeth? I don't understand

— my son has not made the acquaintance of this young lady.'

'Has he not? It was she that he attempted to compromise into an unwanted marriage. Not only is she still a schoolgirl, she is not of sound mind, and has the intellect of a small child. If your son had not been so intent on his perfidy he would have known at once he was molesting the wrong young lady.'

Eastham turned the shade of an old sheet, staggered back to his seat and collapsed. 'My God! This is the most dreadful, appalling information. I give you my word, your grace, my lady wife and I had no idea Percy intended to try and trap Lady Sarah. We were shocked but could see no way out, apart from a betrothal, that wouldn't ruin both their reputations.'

Richard felt almost sorry for the man. 'Lady Elizabeth has no concept of adult behaviour, and thought going with your son part of an elaborate game. Fortunately for him, she's already forgotten the incident, and has suffered no lasting damage from being manhandled in that way.'

'I cannot apologise enough on my son's behalf. Believe me, your grace, he will be sent back to our country estate in disgrace, and his allowance for the remainder of the year shall be terminated. He's obviously not old enough to contemplate matrimony if he cannot behave like a gentleman.'

Richard accepted the apology and took his leave. Eastham had promised that his wife would write at once to all her friends, informing them of the true circumstances. This was essential if this evening's visit to the ball wasn't to be marred by unpleasantness.

His future mother-in-law had taken up residence in the house of a family who lived in Hanover Square, no more than a short walk from where he was. He would venture there and see if he could put matters right with her as, until he had, he and his beloved couldn't tie the knot.

As he approached the residence, he saw his quarry emerge from the front door and head in the direction of a waiting carriage. He increased his pace and hoped that he could prevent her leaving. To his astonishment she stopped, waved frantically, and began to almost run towards him in her eagerness to speak.

'My dear boy, I was on my way to see you all. I've been out of Town for a few days and have just got back to hear what happened. It cannot have been Sarah who behaved with such disregard for convention, so I can only suppose it was Beth.'

'Your grace, might I accompany you in your carriage?'

'It's not mine, my boy, but borrowed for the occasion. I cannot for the life of me think why I behaved as I did. You were right to stop me dipping so deep. Can you forgive me for what I said and allow me to come home?'

He stepped forward and took her hands. 'I'd come here with that very purpose. Your daughters miss you. You're an essential part of our family. It's a beautiful day — shall we walk back together and enjoy the sunshine?'

'I should like that above anything, your grace. First I must arrange for my belongings to be returned.'

A footman had been hovering close by, waiting to hand her grace into the carriage, and must have overheard every word. Richard tossed him a silver coin. 'Have her grace's trunks delivered immediately.'

The young man bowed, delighted with his gratuity. 'Yes, your grace. I shall see to it at once.'

He noticed several people turn and smile in their direction as they strolled past. 'I take it that you didn't try and turn any of your friends against us?'

'Of course I did not, I spoke in the heat of anger at being called out for my poor judgement. I have made a vow to myself to never play cards for money again.'

'I'm delighted to hear you say so,

ma'am. Now, to return to the more pressing question of the incident at Vauxhall Gardens . . . ' He quickly explained what had actually happened and how he'd dealt with the crisis. 'I know you didn't wish for Beth's disability to become common knowledge, but I had no choice but to reveal it.'

* * *

'Amanda, come at once to the window. You won't believe what I can see out there.'

'Sarah, it's most impolite to gawp from behind the curtains.' She stood up reluctantly and walked across to join her sister, making sure she was invisible from outside. 'My word, Richard has brought our mother home. They seem on the best of terms. I thought he'd gone to see Lord Eastham. I wonder how he and Mama come to be together?'

'Do you wish me to speak to the

housekeeper? Ask to have Mama's rooms made ready?'

'Her apartment's immaculate and awaiting her arrival, and has been ever since her departure last week.' She knew exactly why he'd made peace with her parent — he was eager to set a date for their nuptials. When she'd agreed to marry him, it had been with the expectation of there being a long engagement. She'd expected to have had at least three months to get to know him and be quite sure she wished to enter into a permanent relationship. It hadn't occurred to her that he'd be able to put matters straight the same day.

Had she made an error of judgement in accepting him at all? Did she really want to become his wife when she'd known him scarcely two months? A truly chilling image filled her mind — that of him plunging his sword into another man's body. He was a killer, a violent man — how did she know he wouldn't turn on her if sufficiently provoked? The thought of sharing her body with a man who had killed for his living filled her with horror — why hadn't she considered the implications before accepting him so readily?

'Excuse me, Sarah, I suddenly feel most unwell. Could I ask you to apologise to our mother for my absence, and thank Richard for reuniting the family?'

With a hand over her mouth, she fled to her apartment and reached the safety of her dressing room not a moment too soon. When the hideous retching had stopped, she didn't protest when Mary helped her disrobe and tumble into bed.

Within the hour a megrim had her in its vice-like grip, and for the next day and a half she was confined to her bed, unable to keep anything down and almost blinded by her headache.

She awoke on the third day well enough to sit up and take stock of the situation. Her maid, having attended her more than once during these unpleasant episodes, kept the curtains drawn.

'My lady, I'll have a bath drawn for you immediately. I've sent the chambermaid to fetch you some tea and toast.'

'Thank you. I should like to wash my hair, so ensure there's sufficient hot water to do so.'

'Yes, my lady. His grace has enquired several times as to your well-being, as have her grace and Lady Sarah.'

'I've no wish to see anyone today. I'm still too unwell to make sensible conversation. Keep all the doors locked until I give you leave to open them.'

If her maid thought this a strange request, she had the sense not to query it. Amanda's stomach clenched and cold sweat beaded her forehead at the thought of what she'd almost committed herself to. Until she was fully recovered and had her wits about her, she'd no wish to speak to anyone about anything.

It was quite possible Richard had already informed her mother and sisters of their plans to marry. How was she going to extricate herself from this betrothal without splitting the family apart again?

However, one thing she'd realised during her confinement to her bed was that she wasn't ready to marry anyone, and certainly not a soldier. What she felt for him was lust, desire — not romantic love — and this was no basis for a marriage. That she could have such improper thoughts about a gentleman surprised her. Had this been the reason that her parents had married so young, and why they'd had little to do with each other after Beth had been born?

She refused the toast when it arrived, but drank the tea gratefully. Whilst the water was being tipped into the hip bath in front of the fire in the dressing room, she had ample time to mull over how she'd got herself into this predicament.

Whatever he wasn't, Richard *was* physically attractive, charming and intelligent, and something about him stirred unwanted feelings in her nether regions. She was fond of him as a person, desired him as a man . . . but wasn't in love with him, didn't have the depth of emotion that would make her marriage successful.

He was in love with her. She had no doubt about this, and it was going to make it so much harder to tell him that she didn't intend to marry him after all. They couldn't continue to live under the same roof — but now Mama was back, there was no necessity for them all to be here to supervise Sarah's debut.

She would take Beth back to the country where they could both be safe. Richard would remain here, life would go on as it should, and it was unlikely that her absence would even be noticed.

Bathing and washing her hair quite exhausted her; once her locks were dry she flopped into bed and demanded that the curtains remained drawn and that she be left in peace.

When a tray was brought to her later that afternoon, she refused the soup and rolls and drank the lemonade. The mere thought of food made her nauseous again. Her head no longer felt as if it was being split asunder by a cleaver, but her vision had yet to return to normal.

The last time she'd been so prostrated by a megrim had been after the death of her dearest father almost three years ago. It was as if her head was filled with feathers and she couldn't form a coherent thought.

She was rudely awakened on the fifth day by Richard lifting her out of bed and carrying her into her sitting room.

'Now, my girl, you will sit there and eat what is put before you. This nonsense has gone on long enough. Your mother and sisters are beside themselves with worry — as am I.'

She blinked and stared at him. He appeared to have aged ten years since she'd last seen him. 'How did you get in here? I expressly asked for the doors to remain locked against intruders.'

'Through the servants' passageway.'

She now noticed there was already a table laid and an appetising array of items placed upon it. The aroma of coffee wafted towards her.

'I would like some coffee — but I have no wish to eat.'

'I don't give a damn what you wish, Amanda. I'm not leaving here until you've eaten, even if I have to feed you myself.'

Having him so close was unsettling, so she had no choice but to do as he bid if she wanted to get rid of him. Her appetite didn't miraculously return but she managed to drink three cups of coffee and eat two slices of dry toast.

'I've eaten. Now please go away, Richard, I'm really not well enough to speak to you at the moment.'

He picked the table up and carried it across the room as if it was of no weight at all. He then returned and pulled up a straight-backed chair so he could sit close to her.

'What has upset you so much that you're refusing to eat or leave your bed?'

Her eyes filled and she shook her head, unable to answer.

'I release you from your promise,' he said. 'I didn't speak to your family, as we'd agreed not to announce our intention to get married.'

His eyes were damp, his expression sad, and for a moment she wanted to deny that this was what was making her so ill.

'Thank you. Do I have your permission to take Beth back to Denchester?' Her voice was little above a whisper, but he heard her well enough.

'I was going to suggest you do so. Miss Westley and your mother are quite capable of overseeing things. I'll remain here. I won't return to the Dower House in June, but move to Radley Manor until the new hall is completed in a year or two.'

He stood up and replaced the chair, brushed her cheek with his fingertips, and then left her to the misery of her own making.

★ ★ ★

Richard had suffered injuries and illnesses, but nothing hurt as much as losing the woman he loved. The thought that his beloved so hated the idea of becoming his wife that she was unable to eat or rise from her bed filled him with anguish.

He'd never marry. Didn't give a damn about providing an heir. If he couldn't have the woman he loved, he'd remain celibate and a bachelor until his last breath.

When, two days later, he returned from a business meeting to find that Amanda and Beth had left without bidding him farewell, he wasn't surprised.

'My dear boy, I've never seen my daughter so laid low. It's a malaise of some sort, but she refuses to see the physician here. She's promised me she

317

will see Doctor Jenkins on her return.'

'The country air will soon restore her health, your grace. I cannot wait to return myself. I find the confines of society not to my taste after my life as a soldier.'

'That's hardly surprising. Do you think you might call me something less formal than *your grace* now that we are friends?'

'You may use my given name. Perhaps I could call you Aunt Ellen? Would that be acceptable?' The pain in his chest was like a knife at the thought that he could have been calling her *Mama* if things had worked out as he'd hoped.

'That will do very nicely, Richard. I have been thinking that after Sarah's ball in two weeks' time I should like to return to Denchester as well. My girls are not happy here without their older sister, and I miss Amanda too.'

'Then you must set things in motion to that end. I don't believe I mentioned that I won't be returning to the Dower

318

House with you. I think it inappropriate that I live under the same roof as three unmarried young ladies, even if I am their guardian. Radley Manor has been prepared for me.'

'Perhaps that will be best — but you will be only a few miles from us and we can see each other often.'

He had no intention of visiting, but now was not the time to mention it. He would do his duty by them, would always be fond of them, but he must make his life elsewhere. Seeing Amanda would be too painful for him. He prayed that with the passing of time he might feel less, but he doubted it.

The next few days were purgatory, but somehow he got through them without revealing his true feelings. He received an update from the country, and was not reassured by the news.

'Aunt Ellen, have you had a letter from Amanda?'

'I've heard nothing at all and am most concerned about it. My daughter is usually most punctilious about such things. Do you think you could send Mr O'Riley down to ensure that everything is well?'

'I'll do that today. I would go myself, but . . . '

She looked at him with compassion, and he knew then that she was aware of his feelings for her daughter.

'I don't know why Amanda ran away from you, dear boy, but she will understand in time that you are meant to be together.'

For the first time in a week he felt a glimmer of hope. 'Did she tell you that I offered for her, and that she accepted but then changed her mind?'

'She said nothing at all on the subject. I'm not blind, I could see that both of you were suffering. I can assure you that you have my complete support and blessing for your union when you eventually become engaged.'

'How long do I leave it before I approach her a second time? I had a letter from Denchester this morning, and it didn't read well. Amanda's not riding Othello, not eating enough to keep a sparrow alive, and is only taking an interest in Beth's well-being, not her own.'

'Then you must go yourself, Richard. You must talk to her and find out why she changed her mind. Until you do so, neither of you will be happy.'

# 17

'Amanda, why are you so sad? Please play with me; Nanny says her bones are aching and she doesn't want to go outside with me today.'

'I'm sorry to hear that, and of course I'll play with you. Shall we walk to the lake and feed the ducks and the fish? If we take the path through the woods, we'll avoid the builders and be perfectly safe. If you go to the kitchen, I'm certain that Cook will give you a basket of stale bread we can take.'

Beth ran off, happy to have persuaded her to put aside her reading and go out to enjoy the lovely late spring sunshine. This past week had been a torment for her. She was being torn apart by conflicting emotions. When she'd first met Richard, she had been quite certain that he wasn't the man for her, that his past ruled out a future for them together.

Now, however, she was beginning to think that being without him in her life might be worse than the alternative. There were thousands of soldiers with wives and families — if those women could accept the bloody duties of their partners, then so, perhaps, could she.

She vacillated from one opinion to another. One moment she was certain she would never change her mind, and the next that she couldn't live without him.

One thing was certain, however: her feelings for him were not that of a sister, and neither were they just driven by physical attraction. She loved him as much as he loved her, and it seemed ridiculous that her squeamishness was keeping them apart.

The sun was warm for the end of April; the trees were in leaf, the birds singing brightly, and her spirits lifted a little.

'Be careful near the water's edge, Beth — remember, the last time we were here you fell in, and you didn't enjoy it one bit.'

Her sister stopped and swung the basket around, sending pieces of bread flying in all directions, much to the delight of the waiting ducks.

'It was horrid and cold and I had a weed in my hair, and my gown was quite ruined and stuck to my legs.'

'Then I'm sure that today you'll be more careful.'

When the basket was empty, Beth was determined to continue the walk and refused to return to the house. No amount of cajoling would persuade her to change her mind. Eventually, Amanda gave in. 'Very well, shall we walk through the woods and pick some bluebells and primroses? You can fill your basket and then take them back and arrange them. Nanny would be happy to have such a gift.'

'I'll do that. I like bluebells and primroses. Will there be any for me to find?'

'Didn't you notice the bluebells on

either side of the path when we walked through the wood to come here?'

'I didn't. I'm a silly girl. Hurry up, Amanda, I want to fill my basket quickly and take it back for Nanny.'

A pleasant half-hour was spent gathering the blooms, and then her sister was happy to run ahead, her basket brimming with blue and yellow flowers. This left Amanda to complete the walk through the woods on her own.

They had only been out for an hour or two, and not walked more than two miles, but suddenly she was light-headed. Her vision blurred; her knees buckled. She staggered towards the nearest tree trunk in the hope that she could brace herself against it and thus remain upright.

Her hands missed the target and, unable to prevent it, she fell forward into the undergrowth and her world went black.

★ ★ ★

Richard travelled at a leisurely pace, and stopped at Chelmsford and Colchester overnight. He had been persuaded by Patrick to have a groom accompany him, and this man carried his bag.

There was ample opportunity to consider how he was going to approach Amanda when he arrived. She obviously now found him repugnant for some reason, and he wasn't sure he wanted to know why this was. That was being quite nonsensical — if he was to marry the woman he loved, he must ask her why she'd changed her mind.

He was on the last leg of his journey when he had a revelation. He'd quite forgotten that, the first day of their acquaintance, he'd appeared stark naked in his window, and she'd seen him. She was a gently bred young lady, and such a sight must have been shocking to her. He urged his gelding into a canter. Knowing the dowager, he was doubtful that her daughters had been told about the intimacies of marriage.

This wasn't something a future husband would be expected to talk about, but his beloved needed to know the details and be reassured that he'd never hurt her in any way. She must understand that lovemaking was a pleasurable pastime for both parties and nothing to be afraid of.

When he clattered into the stable yard, the groom who'd accompanied him dismounted and took the gelding's reins. Richard strolled to the house and let himself in through the side door. As he wasn't expected, there would have been no preparations made.

A footman jumped to attention. 'Your grace, do you wish for refreshments to be sent to your apartment?'

He hid his smile. This was a polite way of saying that the young man thought his master needed to wash the grime of the journey from his person.

'Nothing to eat — I'll wait until dinner — but send something to drink.

Have hot water fetched to me immediately.'

His valet had remained in Town, so he would have to do for himself. He paused at the bottom of the stairs that led to the upper floor, and could hear Beth chattering away to the nanny. There was no sign of Amanda, but he wanted to see her when he was presentable and not in his dirt.

Fortunately, he'd had the foresight to leave a goodly part of his wardrobe behind. Freshly garbed, he went in search of her. She wasn't anywhere downstairs — in fact, not inside at all as far as he could see. He headed to the nursery, not unduly worried at this point, to speak to Beth.

She flung herself into his arms and he returned her embrace. 'Look, look what I picked for Nanny.'

There were several vases of bluebells and primroses, and he admired them. 'They're quite beautiful, sweetheart. How clever of you to arrange them so prettily. I'm looking for your sister. Do have any notion where she might be?'

'She was walking in the woods with me, but I came on ahead of her.'

'How long ago was that, Beth?'

'I don't know the time. Nanny, have I been back for long?'

The elderly lady stood up, her face showing her concern. 'It's more than two hours ago, your grace. Lady Amanda should have been back by now.'

'Then I'll go and find her for myself. Don't look so worried, little one, I'm sure she's just enjoying the sunshine and the solitude.'

He took the stairs two at a time and ran at the double to the woods that divided the grounds of the Dower House from the Hall.

It was darker under the trees, and cool. He stopped and listened but could hear nothing apart from bird-song and the occasional rustle of a small animal in the undergrowth. He cupped his hands around his mouth and yelled her name. The noise sent birds flapping into the air, squawking their protest at this rude interruption of their peace.

He yelled again, and again got no response. He was seriously concerned now that she'd met with an accident. Hadn't the last letter sent by the housekeeper reported that Amanda was neither eating nor sleeping properly since her return?

He wasn't over-fond of canines, but now wished this family kept dogs. They would find her more quickly than he could. He jogged along the path, looking from side to side for evidence that the girls had passed this way. He stopped every so often and called, but got no response.

He'd been searching for almost an hour without success. He would have to return and organise the staff as he wasn't going to find her on his own. Then, as he turned, he saw a flash of yellow on the far side of the path. He was across in seconds. His heart all but stopped. Spreadeagled, still as death, facedown in the dirt, was his darling girl.

★  ★  ★

Amanda could hear someone calling her, but couldn't find the energy to sit up and answer. She was so comfortable where she was: the soft dirt made an excellent bed, and she hadn't slept for days. She turned her head and settled back into a deep sleep.

The next thing she knew, she was being scooped up into Richard's arms.

'Darling, sweetheart, speak to me. Are you hurt?'

His frantic calls finally dragged her from the land of Nod. 'I'm perfectly well, I just want to sleep. Leave me alone.'

'Idiot girl! I've been searching for hours thinking you'd met with an accident, whilst you were just sleeping.'

Then she was in the air and he was striding back to the house with her clasped to his chest. Having never been carried by anyone since she was out of leading strings, she rather enjoyed the sensation. She was vaguely aware of a fluttering of maids and footmen around her, but was then unceremoniously dumped onto her bed.

'Your clothes are sodden — your maid will get you changed, and then we must talk. I'll wait in your sitting room.'

Her limbs were heavy, her eyes refused to stay open, and Mary slipped a nightgown over her head rather than a fresh gown.

'Let me sleep, I'm so very tired. I'll eat when I wake.' She closed her eyes and was instantly, deeply asleep.

★ ★ ★

It was dawn when she eventually opened her eyes. The shutters and curtains were drawn, and the room was dark. She was about to jump out to find the commode when something stopped her. After her eyes became accustomed to the gloom, she saw that she wasn't

332

alone. Richard was asleep in a chair beside her bed. He was unshaven, looked positively rakish, and the ice around her heart began to melt.

Carefully, she moved to the far side of the bed and tiptoed to the dressing room. When she returned he was still asleep and she paused to look at him. What was he doing here? She wasn't at all unwell. It was a mystery as to why he'd thought it necessary to spend the night in here with her.

She was ravenous, and even the kitchen maids wouldn't be downstairs yet. There was only one thing for it: she would put on her dressing robe and go down to find herself something to eat before she fainted away for a second time from lack of sustenance.

Her hand was on the door when he spoke from the chair, making her squeak with shock.

'If you think I'm going to allow you to parade around the house as you are, you have another think coming. I suggest that you get back into bed at once and allow me to fetch you a tray.'

'I'll do no such thing. You don't know where anything is in the kitchen, and you would take far too long. I haven't eaten for days — that's why I fainted.'

He was on his feet so swiftly she scarcely had time to react. Without a by-your-leave he picked her up and carried her back to bed. 'Stay where you are, young lady, I'll not be long.'

Although his words were softly spoken, there was an edge of steel to them, and she knew it would be unwise to argue on this occasion. She dozed against the pillows and was roused by the delicious smell of coffee, freshly made toast, and something else she couldn't quite name.

'What have you brought me? Is it ham?'

He put the tray on the sideboard on the far side of the room and then fetched the side table and put it beside the bed. 'Wait and see — I'm a resourceful fellow and quite capable of making us both a decent breakfast.'

Her stomach gurgled loudly and they both laughed. When the tray was put beside her, her mouth watered. Not only were there succulent slices of pink ham but also fried eggs to go with them.

'There's enough here for six people, Richard.'

'Then that's fortunate as I've no intention of going downstairs to fetch anything else.'

By the time they were replete, there was very little left on the table. She looked longingly at the empty coffee jug and smiled her most beguiling smile. With a long-suffering sigh he gathered up the dirty plates and cutlery, piled them on the tray and set out for a second time.

Another young lady would be panicking that because a gentleman had spent the night unchaperoned in her bedchamber, she was thoroughly compromised. Amanda was made of sterner stuff. Nobody, apart from staff, and they were loyal to the core, knew anything about it so it made no never mind to her.

Richard had found her in the woods and fetched her home, and then watched over her all night to see that she was safe. The fact that he'd been a serving soldier, had fought in many battles, killed dozens of men, no longer seemed so important.

Being an officer was an important job, for without them leading their men, tyrants and dictators would run rampant across the world. Had it been this that had frightened her into reneging on her promise, or something else entirely?

He returned with a fresh jug of coffee and refilled her cup.

'That was the most delicious meal I've ever eaten. I don't think I knew what real hunger was until today. Thank you for your kindness and for bringing me home. I fear I would have remained there fast asleep if you hadn't come.'

'I doubt you'd have come to any serious harm, my love; the staff would have come out before it got dark and found you eventually. I'm just glad I arrived here when I did and saved you from an unpleasant experience.'

'Why are you here, Richard?'

'I received a letter telling me you weren't eating or sleeping, and I wished to talk to you, see what was bothering you so much that it was affecting your health.'

He was looking at her in a particular fashion, and a wave of heat settled in a most unusual place.

'I can tell you why I've been so distressed. I decided when I first met you that, charming as you are, I could never marry a man who'd killed for a living. I accepted your offer, and then realised I couldn't go through with it.'

* * *

'And now? Have you had time to reconsider? I know that you love me as much as I love you, and it seems

337

ridiculous that your scruples are keeping us from being happy.' She wouldn't meet his eyes, and he knew this was the time to broach the subject of what took place between man and wife in the intimacy of the marriage bed.

'Sweetheart, I don't think it's the fact that I'm a soldier — I should say, more accurately, that I *was* a soldier — I believe it was seeing me unclothed that frightened you.'

She raised her head and nodded slightly. 'I think that maybe you're correct. I've never been so shocked in my life.'

'I take it that your mother has never explained to you what takes place on your wedding night?'

'Of course not. She would be horrified at the thought of mentioning something so . . . so unsuitable for an unmarried lady to hear.'

He couldn't hold back his chuckle. 'There would be little point in her explaining it once you *were* married, as you would know the details for yourself.

'There's nothing to be afraid of, my darling. The act of love that takes place between a husband and wife is as natural as breathing, but far more pleasurable. I promise that I'll never hurt you, and you would never be asked to do anything that you didn't enjoy.'

She was silent for several minutes, and he let her mull over what he'd said. Belatedly, it occurred to him that she probably didn't know how the mechanics of it worked.

'Do you want to know exactly what takes place?'

'I certainly do not. Time enough to discover the details when, and if, I ever get married to you — or anyone else.'

This was the outside of enough. He'd thought the matter settled between them after their intimate conversation.

He reached out and removed her coffee cup from her hands, then placed an arm on either side of her shoulders and stared down at her flushed cheeks.

'Do you love me?' She nodded but seemed unable to answer him. 'Then you will marry me.'

'I'm not sure if I want to marry you or anyone just now. I like being an independent young lady, and would be obliged to give that up if I become a bride.'

Before either of them could move, the door flew open and her mother sailed in. 'Not marry Richard? I should think you will, young lady. In fact, I think the sooner the better after what I've just witnessed.'

There could not have been anything more compromising than the scene that his future mother-in-law had witnessed. Even his beloved knew she now had no choice in the matter.

Smoothly, he stood up while still keeping hold of Amanda's hand. 'You may be the first to congratulate us, your grace. We have decided on a June wedding.'

Amanda, instead of agreeing or even protesting, said something else entirely. 'Mama, what on earth are you doing here? Shouldn't you be escorting

Sarah around Town?'

'We all decided that we had had quite enough of city life, and much preferred the countryside. The ball has been cancelled and Miss Westley sent our apologies to all those from whom we had accepted invitations. Our luggage travelled with us, and our trunks are being unpacked as I speak.'

# 18

Richard was unceremoniously bundled out of the room, leaving Amanda to face the wrath of her mother alone. She would much prefer to have this confrontation when on her feet and fully clothed.

'If you would care to wait in the sitting room, Mama, I'll get dressed and then I can join you.'

'No, my dear girl, I shall sit beside you and we will talk in here where we can be private.' She settled her bulk on the chair that had just been vacated by Richard. 'Can I assume that you and he have sorted out your difficulties and are now ready to tie the knot?'

'I know I've no other choice after what just happened, but the truth is that I'm still not sure it's the right thing for either of us. We scarcely know each other, and physical attraction is not a sound basis for a long and happy marriage.'

'Indeed it is not, my dear. However, yours is a true love match, and one would have to be blind not to see it. I know why you hesitate. You're remembering the coolness between your father and I.'

'I am. It's none of my business, so please don't think you have to explain to me.'

'I know you idolised him, Amanda, but whilst I was carrying Beth he set up his mistress in Ipswich. We swore in church to be faithful to each other, and when he so publicly broke those promises it was too much. From that moment on he was no longer welcome in my bed.'

'I'm so sorry. It must have been hard for you.'

'Somehow, it had been easier to accept his infidelities when he kept them in London, but bringing her so close to home was too much.'

Amanda's breakfast threatened to

343

return when she realised the full import of these words. 'Are you saying that the times he took me to London, it was to visit *her*?'

'I'm sorry to shatter your opinion of him, but he took you with him as a smokescreen. He was very fond of you, of course, but the only person he truly loved was himself.'

These were harsh words indeed, and difficult to hear, but it explained so much. 'So that was why he allowed you to gamble as you wished and paid your debts without a murmur?'

'Exactly so. Life is so much easier for a gentleman, my dear — they can take a mistress without fear of being ostracised by their peers. Their word is law both inside and outside the house, and there's nothing we females can do about it.'

Amanda smiled wryly. 'In which case, Mama, why should I get married?'

'Richard is quite different. He is a good man through and through, will never betray you, will protect and love you as you should be loved. He might look like your departed father, but there the resemblance ends.'

'Thank you for sharing these secrets with me. I must get up and go and find Richard. I need to tell him that I've changed my mind and will marry him after all.'

'I hardly think you are in a position to debate the point, my girl, after having him in here all night and then practically in bed with you when I walked in a while ago.'

'He would never force me into anything I didn't want. Whatever you might think, if I didn't care to marry him, then that would be the end of the matter.'

Her mother tutted under her breath, and then left Amanda to the ministrations of her maid. Another young lady might have spent an hour or more getting ready, making sure she looked her best for this auspicious occasion, but all Amanda could think of was finding the man she loved and telling him her feelings.

She scarcely noticed what she was wearing, but trusted Mary wouldn't send her out looking anything but her best. She flew through the house searching for him, but he was nowhere to be found. She paused in the hall, wondering where she could look next. Why wasn't he waiting eagerly for her to join him?

Then she saw him outside on the lawn, staring up at the roof. What was so interesting out there that it had taken precedence over herself? Curious to know, she rushed out without changing from her indoor slippers.

'Richard, what's so fascinating on the roof? I've been looking for you everywhere.'

He turned, and his smile sent fire through her veins. 'My darling, might I politely suggest that you don't yell across the garden like a fishwife in future? It's hardly becoming in my future duchess.'

'Fiddlesticks to that! I shall shout as

much as I want, and there's nothing you can do about it.' This was a remarkably foolish thing to say as his expression changed and in two strides he had her trapped within his arms.

'Is there not?' His mouth closed over hers, and she was transported to a place she hadn't known existed. Any residual doubts evaporated under the heat of their passion. A delightful time later, he raised his head, his eyes dark and his cheeks flushed.

'You were asking me about the roof. There appears to be a cat and her kittens living up there.'

He pointed, and she saw he was correct. As they watched, Mr O'Riley appeared at an attic window with a sack in his hand. After a deal of mewing and yowling, the felines were safely in the bag and he'd returned to the attic.

'That was most entertaining, my love, don't you think?'

'What I think, Richard, is that for the second time I've ruined a perfectly good gown.'

They returned to the house with his arm firmly around her waist, and she was so happy she thought her feet were actually travelling above the ground.

'I forgot to say, I do wish to marry you, and it's nothing to do with my mother or being compromised.'

'Well, that's a relief, as our kiss was witnessed by two dozen outside men and as many inside.' His smile was wicked as he continued, 'If you didn't marry me, my reputation would be gone — and that would never do, as I'm the Duke of Denchester.'

'So you are, my love. Are you still a reluctant duke, or have you come to terms with your new life?'

'I don't give a damn about the title, the estates or the money I inherited. If I hadn't come here, I would never have met you. I love you, and will always do so. We're going to be so happy together.'

'I love you too, and promise I'll be the best wife I can. If we're to get married next month there's so much to plan, and only six weeks in which to do it.'

'The sooner the better, darling girl, for I doubt I'll be able to stay out of your bed any longer than that.'

We do hope that you have enjoyed reading this large print book.

Did you know that all of our titles are available for purchase?

We publish a wide range of high quality large print books including:
**Romances, Mysteries, Classics**
**General Fiction**
**Non Fiction and Westerns**

Special interest titles available in large print are:
**The Little Oxford Dictionary**
**Music Book, Song Book**
**Hymn Book, Service Book**

Also available from us courtesy of Oxford University Press:
**Young Readers' Dictionary**
**(large print edition)**
**Young Readers' Thesaurus**
**(large print edition)**

For further information or a free brochure, please contact us at:
**Ulverscroft Large Print Books Ltd.,**
**The Green, Bradgate Road, Anstey,**
**Leicester, LE7 7FU, England.**
**Tel:** (00 44) **0116 236 4325**
**Fax:** (00 44) **0116 234 0205**

# NEVER TO BE TOLD

## Kate Finnemore

1967: Upon her death, Lucie Curtis's mother leaves behind a letter that sends her reeling — she was adopted when only a few days old. Soon Lucie is on her way to France to find the mother who gave birth to her during the war. But how can you find a woman who doesn't want to be found? And where does Lucie's adoptive cousin, investigative journalist Yannick, fit in? She is in danger of falling in love with him. However, does he want to help or hinder her in her search?

# SURFING INTO DANGER

## Ken Preston

All Eden wants to do is roam the coast surfing, at one with the waves and her board, winning enough in competitions to finance her nomadic lifestyle. But first the mysterious Finn, and then a disastrous leak from a recycling plant, scupper her plans. With surfing out of the question, Eden investigates. As the crisis deepens, who can she trust — and will she and her friends make it out alive from Max Charon's sinister plastics plant?

# HIS DAUGHTER'S DUTY

## Wendy Kremer

Upon her father's death, Lucinda Harting learns that she faces an impoverished future unless she agrees to marry Lord Laurence Ellesporte, who reveals that his father and hers had made the arrangement in order to amalgamate the two estates. For her sake and that of the servants, she accepts, though they live mostly separate lives. Until one day when shocking news reaches Lucinda's ears: Laurence has been arrested as a spy in France! Determined to secure his release, she heads to Rouen with Laurence's aunt Eliza, and a bold plan . . .

# SUMMER OF WEDDINGS

## Sarah Purdue

Claire loves her job as a teacher, but always looks forward to the long summer break when she can head out into the world in search of new adventures. However, this summer is different. This summer is full of weddings. When Claire meets Gabe, a handsome American in a black leather jacket and motorbike boots, on the way to her best friend Lorna's do, she wonders if this will be her most adventurous summer yet. Will the relationship end in heartache, or a whole new world of possibilities?